DON ISRAEL

DEMETRIUS WALKER

CONTENTS

DON ISRAEL

Copyrights

ACKNOWLEDGMENTS

Wow, I'm living my dreams. Series number 2. I pray that everyone enjoys this story just as much as you all enjoyed the Roc series. Before I get into my acknowledgments, I would like all my readers to know that the books will keep coming. Series after series.

First and foremost, I'd like to thank my beautiful wife, Samantha, for pushing me and encouraging me to finish my stories. She's my biggest cheerleader next to my wonderful mom Angela Johnson. If there was no her, there couldn't be me.

Once again, I have to thank the homie Author God Son. Everything in life happens when it's supposed to and homie you are right on time. Because time and time again, I kept feeling like my books weren't going anywhere. You came along and showed me how to get my stories out and into the world.

Ryan Issca. My boy. You proofread my stories and also encouraged me to sell myself. Blogging about every step it took me to complete my book.

Shout out to the rest of my family. Shout out to my brother Collins Walker and his wife, Tonya Walker. Shout out to my three best friends Abdul (Kama) Olawale, Darrian (Peanut) Mobley, and Antwon (Roni) Ward. Y'all boys have been by my side through more than most.

I can go on and on for days. Shout out to all my classmates from Booker T. Washington HS in Miami, Florida. Shout to my hood Over Town, Miami. We're definitely on an uprise.

PROLOGUE

Just twenty minutes ago, Elihu Israel was announced the first round first draft pick to the Miami Dolphins. $78,000,000,00 contract, with $38,000,000,00 upfront guaranteed. Just like that, he was the richest person that he knew. Now he's able to stand true to everything that he promised his mother and father.

All he wanted to do now was party like a rock star. Driving down 441 doing 120 mph in his new BMW 745I. Using his left hand to hold the loud blunt of weed. Barely holding on to the steering wheel while trying to balance his cup of Patron. In his lap was some white chick that he only met fifteen minutes ago at his draft party. His face had been all over the news and social media for being the highest-ranked middle linebacker in history. In one season, he averaged over 30 sacks and 47 tackles for loss. He broke every defensive record at the University of Miami.

Cutting through traffic like he was a madman behind the wheel. 21 years old and worth over $30,000,000,00 made him feel like he was untouchable. Coming up on his turn, he tried to break the car down, dropping the cup of liquor on the white chick head, causing her to bump her head into the steering wheel. Panicking about not being able to make the turn, he decided to take his chances by going straight through the now red light.

"Bitch, move!" He shouted while trying to gain control of the car. There was nothing he could do but brace himself for impact as the black on black Lincoln town car barely made a complete right turn in front of him. Smashing down hard on the breaks, while he held on tightly to the steering wheel for dear life. Clinching his teeth together as his car seemed to rip the Town car in half. His female passenger flew right out of the windshield. On impact, he ended up breaking both hands and wrists. Plus, he busted his head open. Before blacking out, he noticed the two crushed little white girls in the back seat of the Town car.

"Mr. Israel, I'm sentencing you to 15 mandatory years in Federal prison." Said, Judge Smith.

"This bastard killed my beautiful daughters, and he only gets 15 years. It's fucking murder. He should be doing life." The Italian man shouted out angrily from his seat. His eyes were bloodshot red as if he hadn't slept in days. "I'll kill that nigga myself if I ever see him on the fucking streets again. You dead nigga."

"Mr. Royce, one more word and I will have you removed from the courtroom, and one more slander word, and I'll have you placed in a cell for a couple of hours."

Elihu looked back at the disappointed father of the little girls. The crowd full of white people was giving him the evil eye. In one accident, he killed three white people. He knew that for his actions, he deserved over fifteen years. In one single night, he ruined his whole life.

In the crowd were his parents and his baby mother. The three of them had tears running down their faces. He couldn't look his baby mama in the eyes. She was only 2 months pregnant when he got into the deadly accident. He'll never have the chance to raise his twins from birth, due to the 15 years that he has to serve first.

After signing off on the prison time, he was escorted to the cell then he'll be shipped off to the federal prison. In the holding cell, he dropped his head into his hands. Refusing to let anyone see him cry or shed a single tear, he sat up straight. Thinking to himself that he'll be 36 years old when he touches the street again. Never in a million years would he have thought he'll make it to the NFL and not get to play a single snap. He was the best linebacker to ever put on a jersey, and he will never have a chance to prove it to the world.

"Elihu Israel, can I get your autograph. No one ain't going to believe that I was the bailiff in your case without it." The female Bailiff asked while holding out a pen and a Miami Dolphins poster with his picture on it.

He wanted to tell her to get the fuck away from him, but he signed it anyway. He made his way back to his seat, then waited patiently for his name to be called, so he could be shipped off to downtown. After what seemed like hours, his ride had finally arrived. Once he was cuffed from behind, he was escorted out of the building and into a black Chevy Tahoe.

On the ride, he made sure to get a good look at everything that they road pass. Pulling up to the Feds, he took a deep breath. If he had to serve time, he'll rather do it around people with real money, then be in state prison with a whole bunch of street hustlers and want to be gang members.

"Welcome to MCI. This will be your home for the next 15 years unless you do something stupid enough to get you shipped far away from home. Once you stepped foot out of that truck, whoever you were out the gate doesn't matter here. You're an inmate now until you get released. Now strip inmate Israel." Screamed the little correction officer.

Elihu said a silent prayer for himself. If all the correction officers were like this one, it was sure to be a long 15 years. His prison sentence will either make him or break him, but only time will tell.

CHAPTER ONE

Today marked the end of Elihu prison sentence. Throughout his term in prison, he saw more bloodshed and violence then imaginable. He overcame a few problems that came his way also. He refused to let anyone kill him while behind bars. Knowing that the Italian would stand true to his word, he made sure to back the hitmen up who came his way that tried to take his life.

Sharing a cell with Mexican Gus paid off for him, but it only brought him beef with the rival Mexican gangs. While working out on the rec yard, he saved Gus's life from a potential hit. Proving his loyalty, and the fact that he didn't fear death, the Dominguez Cartel accepted him as if he was one of their own.

Stripping his sheets off the bunk and rolling up the mattress, he was ready to enter the free world again. The only thing that he was taking home with him was his picture book. Everything else he was leaving with Gus.

"What's the first thing you doing once you walk out of those gates, Elihu?" Gus asked as he stood by the door with three other Mexicans. He was trying to remain strong. Over the last three years, they became more than homies. They became brothers.

"I haven't thought about that yet. Might just enjoy myself a home-cooked meal from my mother. That's if she feels up to it."

"inmate Israel you can stay if you want. If not, you need to come on. Your time is up." The dorm officer yelled over the loudspeaker. He was starting to get fed up with Elihu. That was his third time calling for him over the loudspeaker.

"Come on. It's time for you to ride, brother." Gus was having a hard time dealing with the fact that his brother was going home. They had become extremely close to each other. For months he dreaded this day, and finally, it came. Grabbing Elihu as they embraced in a brotherly hug. "If you ever need anything, contact this person or just look her up if you ever in Mexico. Comprende?"

"I understand." He replied while placing the small piece of paper in his pocket.

Giving dap to the rest of his Mexican homies as he made his way out of the dorm. Once he got to the visitation room, he was allowed to change into the regular civilian clothes that his family brought for him to be released in. Wasting no time, he ripped the prison uniform off, then got dressed in the Gucci linen, and matching red bottoms. The expensive clothing made him feel like a million bucks again.

Standing behind the metal door as they slowly opened it up for him, he noticed the crowd of nosy reporters trying to get the first story. Before stepping out like a free man, he took a deep breath, then stepped out on his right foot first, and never turning around to look at the building. In the mix of the crowd, he saw his sister standing there with a smile on her face. The whole time he was locked away, she never missed a beat for him. He made her power of attorney over $15,000,000.00 of his money. Judging by the Bentley truck that she had parked out front, she has done real good with his money.

"Israel..... Israel.... What's next for you now that you're free?" One of the reporters yelled out while they all awaited his response.

"I'm going to spend some time with my family. Now can you guys move so we can get out of here? "He asked while climbing in the passenger seat. Once he shut the door, everything they were saying seemed to have drowned out.

"Welcome home, brother. Get brushed up on this while we head to mother's house." Kimberly said while placing the large envelope on his chest. "I didn't even use the whole $15,000,000.00 that you gave me. Using under seven million dollars, I opened three high rises, two-car lots, and I started our own record label. 1700 Records." She handed him a platinum iced out chain with the 1700 logo flooded with diamonds.

"You did real good. Say's here that you turned 7 million dollars into 42 million dollars. You can continue to control all of the businesses. I have something up my sleeve that will put us on a whole different level. I just have to keep a low profile right now. The media and the Feds will be on my trial for a while. So for right now, I just want to be around family. I'm proud of what you did, though, Kim. The NFL has been sending all types of threats my way about the guaranteed money that I got upfront without stepping one foot on the field. I earned every dollar that had been giving to me."

"It's no secret that if the accident never happened, you would've dominated the pros. They can send all the lawyers they want or even try to sue. They can't take a single dollar from you." Over the years, she had her fair share of run-ins with the NFL and their lawyers about her brother and his money.

"How's Lisa? I haven't heard from her since my court date 15 years ago. I wrote to her and wrote, just to never get a response." He knows that he messed up. He should've never cheated on her. The way it came out was just too much for anyone. He killed the woman that he was cheating with. He had too many regrets about that night.

"She got married, Elihu. She has been married for 9 years now. She met someone two years after you left; they have three kids together. I set her up to a point she would be straight. All she has to do is maintain the business. I started her with 6 big rigs. Now she's up to 30 rigs on the road. Doing deliveries for some major companies. She has plenty of potentials to grow even bigger. That was enough money to set everyone straight. Plus, you're able to come home and make any move you want." She explained while pulling in the gated property.

After pulling away from the gate, the two-story house must've set a half-mile away from the main road. In front of the White House with red trimming was 5 other luxury vehicles. Benz's, Bentleys, and two

Rolls Royces. He almost shed a tear. When he was a free man, his family was poor and struggling. He abused his body on the football field, so his family didn't have to worry about a thing again in life. The driveway alone assured him he had done the right thing.

Climbing out of the truck while checking out his surroundings. He was delighted with what his money could buy. Locking arms with his beautiful sister, as she led the way into the 10 bedrooms 6 bathroom house.

"Welcome home!" His family shouted out once he stepped foot in the house.

"Welcome home, son." Said his father, Anthony Williams Sr, while embracing his oldest son in a tight hug.

"It feels good to be home, Pops. I missed Y'all like crazy. I'm just glad that you and mama are still around."

"Where we going, boy. You act like we old as dirt." Ms. Williams playfully said while slapping him on the arm. She stood there for a moment and took everything about her son before she wrapped her arms around him. He was standing there all toned up. He stood at 6'6, 260 lbs. From the lack of sunlight, his once jet black skin was now a dark brown. His eyes were white, she could only imagine how much longer before they turn red again. His dreadlocks hung to the small of his back, and his beard hung down to his chest. He could pass as a Hebrew now.

"I told you you'll be the one to change lives. You have become the man that you wanted to be. Now take back everything those white people have taking from us for so many years. You are a God. Nothing happens if you don't allow it. So stand on all ten toes. You will move mountains, my son. Them crackers tried to break you. That system only made you a lot smarter and sharper. Now come and give me some love. I love you, my son." She didn't even try to stop the tears from falling. The tears she is shedding will be the last tears she'll ever shed for him.

After hugging his mother for a moment, he hugged his brother, then finally faced his twins for the first time in all of their lives. His son reminded him of his self when he was 14 years old. His beautiful daughter took after her mother, but she had his complexion. For what seemed like hours, they just stared at each other. Mr. And Mrs. Williams looked on, hoping that the kids will forgive their father for going to prison before they were even born.

Erica stepped forward first, then Eric was right behind her. They both latched on their father for the first time ever. His arms were so big, he didn't have a problem hugging them both at the same time. Pulling away from them after a moment while taking in their faces.

"I'm sorry for being so reckless, but I can promise you both that your father is here to stay. I can't make up for the years we lost, but I can make sure that our future is great. As Y'all father, I will be here for you both every step of the way."

"Son dinner will be ready shortly. You three can go out back and get better acquainted." Ms. Williams suggested while moving the rest of the family along, trying to give the three their privacy.

Elihu grabbed both of his kids by the hands, then lead them outside to the patio area. They had so much to learn about each other. He figured that he'll get them alone and just talk with them.

CHAPTER TWO

Too many years have passed by, and Don Robert Royce still hasn't found peace with the death of his daughters. After their accidental death, he slipped into a deep depression for a couple of years. For years he blamed himself for not allowing the girls to ride in the limo with himself, and his wife, Carla. They begged him to let them ride alone.

There was no way he could bury them, so he had them both cremated. He refused to change anything about their bedroom. All of their things were in the same spot that they left them in since the night they died. Setting on the shelf was both of their urns and pictures of them both.

Most Mornings, he starts his day off by spending time with them both. Precisely the same thing he once used to do before they passed. Holding onto both of their favorite pink teddy bears as if they were his actual daughters. With all the money in the world, a man can ask for, but it's not enough to bring them back.

"Robert!" Carla hated to interrupt him, but she needed him to come and take a look at the television. "You have to come and see the news." She worried about her husband. Since the new year came in, he had been acting strangely.

After kissing both teddy bears, he placed them where the girls had left them, then rushed into the living room behind his wife. What he saw on Fox local news was the headline he had been looking for all year. He knew that it wouldn't be long after the new year came in that the man that killed his daughters would be released. For too many years, he planned so many different ways to kill him. Now that he's released from prison, he can set his plan in motion.

"Boss, the men found Mike. They're taking him to the slaughterhouse right now as we speak. I have the car running for you already." Ralph thought Don Royce would be glad to know that they finally tracked down Mike. After shutting up for a moment, he realized what had Don Royce's full attention. Looking at the news himself, watching the camera crew follow Elihu and a woman to a snow-white Bentley truck. Knowing how tough things are right now for his boss, so he decided to give him his space.

Don Royce stood there in the same spot until the news switched to another topic. He was beyond pissed. He paid good money to know when Elihu would be released, just for him to walk out of prison without a care in the world. He wanted to be the first face that he saw when the gates closed behind him, and the last face he saw once he took his life.

His Jewish lawyer owes him big time for not doing what he paid him for. He grabbed his Kangal hat, dusted it off then placed it on his head. Standing in the doorway, he hugged his beautiful wife real tight then kissed her on the lips. "I love you. I promise to bring you this nigga head on a platter."

"I love you too, and I know without a shadow of a doubt that you'll do just what you say. But can you promise me you won't touch him anytime soon? Because if you make a move right now, the law will be all over you. There's no way that I can live without you as well. Move-in these Miami streets like you had when we first moved here from Boston." She fixed his collar shirt, then plucked a couple pieces of lint from his coat.

His mind had been wrapped around the death of their two daughters for so long, he never noticed the fact that they both were getting older. Brushing her salt & pepper hair behind her ear while looking into her sad red eyes. Every time he steps out the door, there's a chance that he'll never step back in the house. His lifestyle only added to her worries.

"I'm a Don. Miami is my city. I can do as I please, but I'll respect your wishes." He hated to see her worry about anything. After losing their daughters, they tired multiple times to have kids again. Due to their age, Carla could never hold a child again. At times like this, all he knew to do was give her enough money to go shopping. Pulling out a knot of hundred dollar bills. "Take this and buy you something nice." He said while handing her the large lump sum of cash.

She could care less about his money right now. She needed him to move smartly. A man with his status was at the top of everyone's hit list. "just be careful out there. Lately, you ain't been thinking straight. Don't let this man that killed our kids blind you from what's really going on. Make sure that everyone knows that Don Robert Royce is the Boss of all Bosses. You come second to no one."

Her words always seemed to move him. Feeling a lot better and ready to face the world, he kissed her lips, then headed out the door to his running car that awaited him. His driver held the back door open for him as he approached the platinum-colored Rolls Royce. Before taking his seat in the back, he waved goodbye to his wife as she stood in the double doorway with her arms crossed under her breast. She replied to his wave with a simple smile. He never took his eyes off of her until his car was out of eyesight.

"Hey, what's going on?" Federal Agent Rashonda Coleman asked another female agent. Everyone looked to be rushing into the conference room, and she had no idea what was going on. She was new to the Miami office. Just recently, she transferred down south because of a bust that went terribly wrong and almost cost her life.

"They're looking for two people to cover a new assignment." The agent explained to her, then rushed inside the conference room herself.

Rashonda figured that she'll stand in the back and just see what's all the fuss about. She took her place against the back wall just before the meeting started.

"Ok, everyone, settle down. Today's topic is about the Dominguez Cartel. We believe that the subject Elihu Israel can and will lead us to the source who is the head of the dangerous cartel, and crime family. Yes, Elihu is a black man. He's the only black man allowed to spend not one night but three years in the cell with Gustavo Dominguez. We all know that Gus is a well-respected family member in the Dominguez family. Word is that Elihu and Gus became like brothers in that cell. They both even saved each other lives. Don Royce men were found dead in prison after attempting to murder Elihu. He returned the helping hand when a rival Mexican cartel gang member tried to stab Gus to death only for Elihu to help him take out the rival. For as long as we been following the Dominguez Cartel, we could never find as much as a leak in their family. Elihu might be our last chance to infiltrate their organization because we all know that black people will snitch before going back to prison-"

She heard everything he was saying, but what he wasn't saying is that Elihu was a free man and that they don't have anything on him. "Excuse me, sir, if I may cut in."

"Agent Coleman, right?"

"Yes, Sir. Elihu Israel is a rich man. I don't see any need for him to do business with the Cartel. If I was released from prison with over $20 million, why would I want to do business with drug dealers? Isn't the objective for the local drug dealers are to make a couple million dollars then get out the game before we can catch on to them?" She needed him to make this idea that he has to make sense to her.

The leading agent stood at the podium with a smile on his face. This is why his division can use someone like agent Coleman, he thought. She had no problem asking questions. Everyone else would just sit there and listen to him speak. Not understanding anything that he was saying, so they'll end up calling him all times throughout the night and day trying to figure out what he asked of them. "Thanks to Elihu's sister Kimberly he stepped out of prison a very comfortable man. But let me tell you all something about Elihu. He's the type of man that wants more for black people. Born Anthony Williams, he changed his birth name because he feels like he's the missing link to black people taking back what's owed to them. Him making it to the NFL was just a stepping stone. While serving time, he taught classes on Hebrew Israelites. At one point, he had over 300 inmates change their religion. Some of the inmates believed that he was God in the living flesh. The money that he has is not going to be enough for the things he's trying to do. This is why we need to get close to Elihu. Gustavo believed in whatever Elihu was teaching, so I'm willing to bet he will plug him in with the Cartel. Plus, the Cartel can use someone like Elihu to move their cocaine."

Agent Coleman could see where the leading agent was going with things now. The amount of money that he could make off Cocaine was enough to get his Hebrew movement started. Plus, how good Kimberly was with flipping money, he could easily cover it all up.

Once the meeting came to an end, she made her way to her office and took a seat behind the desk. Logging into her apple laptop, she decided to look up Elihu Israel. The headline was of his release from jail today. Next was a terrible accident that took three people's lives. Looking into his prison rap sheet, it was squeaky clean. There weren't any records of him ever going to lock up. Digging deeper, she found something. A couple of female officers were fired because of them trying to show him special treatment. Word was that Elihu turned down each of their advances. She wanted to think he may have been gay, but after looking over a couple of pictures of his set of twins, and their beautiful mother. Blowing up his picture, allowing her to get a good look at him, she could see why the women were throwing themselves at him. He was a very handsome dark skin man.

"Knock knock, do you mind if I step in for a moment?" Asking the division Leader as he stood there in her doorway.

"Come right on in." She replied while clicking off Elihu's case. "What do I owe for you stopping by my office?"

"Well, I want you to go undercover and cover this Cartel thing for me. Someone with your expertise can easily crack this one for me. If you can pull it off, I'll make sure you get that special agent promotion that you been working for. You just one big bust away. So what do you say?" He asked while giving her his signature puppy dog look.

"I want my promotion." She said while pointing at his face.

"Great, so this means you'll take this case. For that, you can pick your own team. You leading this case. I know you going to make me proud. Give me an hour, and I should have everything emailed to you." He was excited that the ball was about to get rolling on the Dominguez Cartel countdown until they arrest them all. He walked out of her office, singing one of his favorite songs by 2 Chains.

She just shook her head while laughing at her boss. She would have never thought the old white man even knew that song, or even who 2 Chains was. All she could think to herself was how better the Miami office is over The Atlanta office. Even if her last boss asks her to return, she'll turn the position down to stay in Miami. Now that she has a new case, she made room by cleaning up her desk, making room for her latest investigation. None of the dealers or major players didn't have any idea who she was so she can move through the streets; however, she saw fit. Clearing off her drawing board as she readied herself for this case. The streets of Miami didn't have a single idea about the Pitt Bull in the skirt suit was about to roam the streets.

CHAPTER THREE

After spending time with his family, renewing his driver's license, and registering with the Miami-Dade Police department, he headed over town in his new white Bentley truck. The limo tinted windows were dark enough to keep onlookers from looking in his truck as he rode around his old stomping grounds. The luxury truck demanded everyone's attention. Nothing seemed to have changed about his old neighborhood. Dope fiends still could be found slobbing out the mouth outside the neighborhood corner stores. Young teens were still riding up and down the blocks on bicycles while looking out for cops or anyone that looked out of place. The corner hustle usually pays the teens a little of nothing to watch out for the police for them.

While passing through, he spotted a couple of people that went to high school with him. He came to a stop after seeing 2 little girls playing in the streets. The youngest one couldn't be any older than 3 years of age. Climbing out of the truck, then he waved for them both to come over to him.

"Where's Y'all, mother?" He asked them out of concern. It was nothing for someone to turn the corner of 2nd court and 13th street doing at least 40 mph trying to show out in a rental car, or a stolen one. The youngest one didn't have any clothes or shoes. Dressed in only a soiled pull-up.

"She's in the house sleep." Said the oldest one noticing that she was in trouble.

"How old are you?"

"Four. I'm in trouble?"

Elihu couldn't believe how these beautiful little girls were able to be playing in the road without someone saying something. There were all types of broken glass and other sharp objects that could cut these little girls' feet. "Take me to your mother?" He was beyond upset. If they were his kids, he'd want to kill his kid's mom.

The youngest one grabbed him by the hand and pulled him towards their mom's apartment. Just as they stepped on the porch, a young gentleman greeted them. He also looked like he could use a good meal and a couple of dollars for a haircut, and some clean clothes. The hand-cut short jeans he was wearing looked to be too small for his tall frame.

"Y'all get in the house. And what I told y'all about talking to strangers?" He snapped while trying to look tough in front of the strange man that stood in his doorway.

"What's your name, kid?"

"My name doesn't matter. Who you? Some type of social worker or something. If you are, we don't need any help."

"David, who is that at my door?" The mother of the house asked after hearing the commotion coming from the door.

"Nobody, mom, he was just leaving. You can go lay back down."

The woman of the house pushed her son out of the way and took a good look at the gentleman standing there. She couldn't believe her eyes. All this morning, the news had been airing his release from prison. "David, this man isn't just no anybody. This is Anthony Williams, aka Elihu Israel. How you been friends?" For a second, she didn't realize who was at her door. When it hit her, it hit like a ton of bricks. She was now embarrassed. Trying to cover up her ugliness due to all the years she had been doing drugs.

Looking through her roughness, he could see his childhood friend underneath the bags under her eyes and her missing teeth. "I stopped by because the kids were playing in the streets. You need to get the landlord to fix the string door. This ain't no street to have little girls running around barefoot."

"Anthony, is that you?" Another woman asked from two apartments down.

"Yea, who that?" He replied. He figured that the Bentley truck was causing everyone to come and see what was going on.

He found himself hugging and speaking to people he hadn't seen or heard from in years. Digging inside the book bag sitting on the passenger side of his truck, he pulled out a couple thousand dollars that he was riding around with. He called David over to him. "Hey, take this money and buy some things for your family. You have to be the man of that house. Make sure you get a cell phone also. Call me at this number as soon as you get a phone. I'm offering you a job as my driver. All you got to do is drive. You have your driver's license, right?"

David couldn't believe his eyes. In his 20 years of life, he had never seen this much money. "I'll take the job. I will call you first thing in the morning."

"Make sure you call me. Every man should be able to take care of his mother and family." Elihu explained to him, then allowed him to run off in the house. Pulling out some more money, he gave every kid on the block a hundred dollar bill. Growing up, Overtown himself, the hustlers of his generation, always gave back to the hood. He had big plans for his hood. In due time he would clean it all up. After running out of money, and taking pictures with everyone that he knew, he climbed back in his truck with one more stop in mind for today.

* * * * *

"Listen here, punk. I'm not going to ask you one more time. If you don't want me to kick in your grandmother's door and kill everyone in there eating Sunday dinner this weekend, you better tell me where that money at?" He was growing impatient with his latest victim. Sticking up corner hustlers, and robbers were his new come up.

Just recently, he lost his mother, and things went belly up right afterward. Kidnapping the hustlers and robbers didn't pay much, but this one was at the top of the food chain. He wanted his life more than he wanted his money because he liked to have sex with the young teenage girls in the hood.

The windowless room was covered in plastic. While his victim hung upside down from the ceiling. He had already been beaten severely. A few blows to the ribs with a household hammer broke his ribs on the left side. He had to admit the kid was tough. Picking up a knife from his plastic-covered table. "You still ain't trying to tell me?" He asked while grabbing him by the nuts then stretching them out. He placed the cold blade of the knife against his nuts. "You got 5 seconds, then I'm cutting them off." He started the countdown.

"Goddamn... ok, man. Just don't fucking kill me. The money is in the trunk of my beat up, Caddy behind my crib." He was starting to become light-headed from being upside down for so long. "Cut me down, man."

Without a second thought, he cut his victim down, then tied him up to a metal chair. "If the money ain't there, I'm going to make a stop by Grandma's house in Opa-Locka." He told him while tapping him on the chest with the knife.

"Man, the money is there. And don't fuck with my family."

"I call the shots, not you playboy." He said while gagging his victim. While he's gone, he doesn't need anyone stumbling on to him.

Making his way upstairs to the ground floor, then he locked the steel door behind him. Standing at the door, he stripped out of his monkey suit and water boots. Folding everything up and placing his things right outside the door. Feeling like something was out of place, so he quickly turned around with his gun in his hand. Who he saw standing there damn near blew his mind.

"It been 15 years already?" He asked his good friend, noticing him standing there in the flesh.

"Yes, it has my brother. I see you still up to your same tricks. Who you got down there. A hustler, or a Robber?"

"He's a hustler. A soon to be dead hustlers that like little girls. The hood will be a better place without him. But enough about him. Welcome home, Elihu."

"It feels good to be back out here with loved ones. But you already know why I'm here. In a couple more days I'm going to take that trip to Mexico. If you want, you can slide with me. For now, handle that situation you have downstairs, then lay on me to reach out to you. I'm really about to step things up a notch. Oh, yea, do me a sold, track down Snoop and let him know that I said it's on."

"Bruh, you just walked out of the gate. You sure you don't want to spend some time with your kids first?" Ethan, aka Venom, asked his good friend. He remembers clearly all of the things they talked about while serving time. The most important one was the talk about taking back what was owed to the black man.

"Just give me a couple of days. The plan changed slightly. You just make sure that Snoop is there. And Venom, you need to stop smoking that shit. That shit will kill you one of these days." Elihu said while looking at the crack pipe sitting on the kitchen counter with a few crack rocks sitting next to it.

Venom couldn't say a thing. His addiction to crack was what keep him going. With all the death he saw overseas fighting the white man war was enough to drive any man crazy. Smoking crack was his escape. Once Elihu was out of the door, Venom picked up a small piece of crack, then stuffed his glass pipe with it. Picking up his lighter, then placed fire to the other end of the pipe. As the rock popped and bowled, he inhaled deeply. The hit of crack was so strong, it knocked out his hearing. One good blast, and he was higher than he ever been. Feeling like he was on top of the world. Tucking his guns, then he left the house behind Elihu.

As of recently, Don Royce had noticed that someone was holding back on his cut of the money. He thought he had made it very clear many years ago that his money was something not to mess with. His men had finally tracked down Mike, the bookie. His job was to run all of Don Royce's number houses.

"You betrayed me and tried to run off with my money. You know the consequences that come with taking from me?" Don Royce was disappointed in Mike. He had known the kid for far too many years, and he never had one problem with him.

"Don Royce, I know it looks like I been stealing from you. I swear I would never touch a single dollar of your money. Someone is setting me up to take the fall. Please, sir, you have to believe me. You know I'll never do this to you."

Don Royce believed the kid for some reason, but everything pointed at him. Each member of his crew had a different job to do. He personally set it up that way so he can keep a record of who was handling what.

Looking around the small closed-in room at the few facing that seemed to be waiting on whatever he tells them to do. All of his men trusted each other. They had been running a legitimate and clean business for many years now. Even that still wasn't enough for Him to spare Mike's life. He hates to have to kill him, but an example has to be set.

Grabbing the knife from the table of weapons, then he turned and faced a now shaking up Mike. "Let this be an example to all of you. No one is above getting killed for my money. I pay you all well, so there should be no reason for any of you to steal from me. Plus, I treat you all like family. I will not tolerate any kind of disrespect for mine." He starred in everyone's eyes that was standing in the room. He needed them all to know how serious he was about killing them all for his money.

"Boss, I swear it wasn't me. I'll never steal from you. Since you made me a part of the family, you never had one problem with me. I'm telling you someone set me up."

His words were not affecting Don Royce because his mind was already made up. Even if he really didn't do it. He had to be used as an example. If he were to let him live, then someone would try it again. "Gag him." He shouted, causing his two personal henchmen to spring into action. One held Mike's mouth open, while the other one gagged him.

By now Mike was crying uncontrollably. His tears didn't move Don Royce at all. He placed the knife just below Mikes left ear, then ran the sharp blade across his throat. His blood splashed while he struggles to catch his breath. A breath that he'll never catch again. As he bleeds to death Don Royce makes all of his men stand there and watch Mike die. After he took his last breath the two henchmen started wrapping him up, Don Royce turned back to the men standing there.

"You know its crazy. I really believed him when he said that he never took from me. I killed him because he wasn't smart enough to see that someone used him. If none of you don't want to share the same faith as Mike, then I suggest that you double count or even triple count my money before you bring it to me even a single dollar short. If you don't value your life then be my guest, and fuck up my money." He gave it a minute to let what he said to them sink in, before allowing them all a chance to leave. Once everyone was gone he walked up to Mikes lifeless body. He was one of his most loyal bookies, and if he couldn't trust him that could only mean that he can't trust anyone. He thought to himself while unconsciously spinning his commission ring.

Things were starting to become strange. First, it was the murder of two of his most trusted undercover Cops. Now someone has taken money from him. Over $40,000.00 gone without a trace. At his old age, he has no strength for an actual war. Back in Boston, most people won't even walk on the same sidewalk if they knew that the mob was coming their way. In Miami, people didn't fear power. His family wasn't in Miami five years when he lost both daughters.

Sometimes he thinks he should've stayed in Boston and fought it out with whoever didn't want to see his family eat. Listening to his lovely wife, he made the move to Miami without anyone knowing that he was moving his family. One part of him wanted to believe that the rest of the Don's has found out he's in Miami. If so he has to prepare himself for one of the biggest battles of his life.

He took one more look at Mikes body then walked out the house hoping that he does have someone stealing from him instead of the Round Table of Dons finding out that he moved to Miami. Since his family moved, and they changed their numbers they haven't heard a thing from any one apart of the commission. He just knew that death would be knocking on his door any day now.

Climbing in the back seat of his car he decided to leave his negative thoughts in the slaughterhouse with Mikes body. He poured himself a glass of champagne, then fired up his Cuban cigar. A nice glass of champagne and the smooth smoke from the Cuban cigar is usually enough to clear his mind. As his car pulled away from the house he was starting to feel better already. Right now all he wanted was to be with his wife. He had the driver step on it. After 2 cups, and smoking the cigar halfway down he was now feeling good. He put the cigar out and set down his empty cup. Don Royce decided to relax, being that he had another 20 minutes before he makes it home. He closed the curtains in the back then rested his head on the headrest. Before he knew it he was out cold.

CHAPTER FOUR

It's been a few days since Elihu came home from prison, and he has not once sat down. He had a choice to make between buying his own home or living in the sizeable house that he brought for his parents. Sitting at the counter as his mother sat him a plate of breakfast down. Things still seemed unreal to him. Most days he has to blink his eyes a few times just to make sure he's not seeing things.

"Son you know that you can live here. Shid your money is what paid for this place. You don't have to rush into anything." Said, Mrs. Williams, as she sat across from him at the bar like table. Looking at his handsome face as he ate her food with a smile on her face. "When you were just a little boy you told me you were going to buy me a big house and that I'll never have to struggle again. I never doubted you son. Now let us take care of you. You just did all that time. You need to find you a wife, and build a bond with those kids of yours. Everything else can wait. You not struggling for money, plus Kim is investing money in all types of assets. Within a few more years this family will be worth over five hundred million dollars. What more do you need?" She knows her son all too well. He came home with that look of hunger in his eyes. She could only hope that she can change his mind from doing anything that could land him back in Prison.

He took another bite of his food then sat his fork down. In his 36 years of life, he's not once lied to his mother and he's not going to start now. After chewing and swallowing his food did he respond to her. "Yes, we have a decent nest egg for me to lay down and live off of the interest money that the banks will be kicking out each year. The problem is that's not enough money for what I'm trying to do. I want to open Rec buildings around the states. Places where black people can go to find jobs, housing, food, and trades. I want to teach our people the things that the white people are selling us. Before slavery, we as black people used to help each other out. We used to Tell a friend how to survive. When the whites stepped in the picture they learned our ways, then started killing our people off. So now we have to buy everything we need. They introduced us to the word "sell." The letter 'S' is of the serpent. I will burn down everything they build, and start back Teaching our people. The only way they'll be able to stop me is with death, and mother I'm not afraid of dying."

Mrs. Williams continued to stare into his eyes. What he was saying would bring a lot of trouble their way. She knows firsthand that some of the things that the white people show you in the movies are true. "We're gonna have to live underground for something like that. When you take money out of the government mouth that's when they come with guns drawn. If they look you way for something, that's when they start killing your family off. Are you willing to risk your family life for some people that like being blinded by material things?"

"I will do everything I can to take back what's belonged to us as Blacks. I have bigger plans then black wall street, and I have over three thousand followers that believe in my movement. So no I can't stay here mother." He pushed his plate away then stood up at the table. "Excuse me Mother and thanks for the breakfast."

Mrs. Williams just looked at her son for a moment before saying another word. "If you going to do it, then do it real big. Throw a monkey wrench in everything that them White people got going on."

"I plan too." He assured her then walked out of the door.

Standing there with the Bentley truck running was David the young kid he hired as his driver from Overtown. His once nappy head was freshly cut, and he was wearing all white from his shirt down to his shoes. He looked like a different person. He was a prime example that enough money can change anyone life.

"Good morning Mr. Israel. Is there any specific place that you'll like to go this morning?" David asked while holding the back door open for his boss as he waited on any orders he have for him.

"Yea take me to this address," Elihu said while handing David a small piece of paper with only an address wrote on it.

David shut the door behind Elihu then ran around the truck and climbed under the wheel. After punching the address in the GPS, he pulled away from the sizeable house. Just a couple of days ago he had no idea how he would get his family out of the hood, now here he is driving an expansive truck and making good money a week. Money that none of the people that went to school with him would make in a week even if they finish college. There was no way that he plans on messing this job up for himself.

Elihu pulled out the piece of paper that Gustavo gave him before leaving prison. The world around the prison yard was that Gustavo was the brother of some Cartel leader. While locked away with him Elihu never questioned him about it. One it wasn't his business and two the way the gang members flocked to his hand and foot was a dead give-away he was somebody. Elihu knew that he was somebody himself, so he could never rock to any other man beat.

Opening the paper, there was a name on it that was very hard to pronounce with an address that had to be in Mexico because he never saw anything wrote like it before. On the back was a message that he couldn't make out. Folding it back up, then he placed it back in his wallet for safekeeping.

Thinking about all the brothers he left behind in prison that's never coming home. The Feds has railroaded to many blacks with drug charges. The crack law alone has over three hundred thousand black men locked away. Just thinking about it was enough to give him a headache.

Once they got to the address Elihu looked at his first property. Parked out front was his sister Kimberly Rolls Royce. He instructed David to park beside her car. She was nowhere in sight so he figured that she must be inside. Before heading inside himself he looked around at the surrounding area. The location couldn't have been better. It was right in the middle of Liberty City. He didn't want it to be out of reach from the people he's trying to help.

Feeling good about the choice of location that Kimberly chose as he walked inside the empty building. The building was 4 stories high and comprised 48 rooms and eight male and female bathrooms on each floor.

"Do you like it, brother? And who's this handsome young man?" She asked while wondering why the young man looked familiar to her.

"I love the layout and the location. Once we fix it up the way that I would like, then we'll open our doors to the public. There is so much that I have to teach our people. Especially our black women. They need to understand why child support is not good for our black men. Changing the way our women think is the first way of saving black lives. Now this young man is David. His mom went to high school with us." He went on to explain the details then he let David fill in the blanks.

"How soon can I get this place furnished? I'm trying to be open asap." What he got planned he feels that everyone can grow from it.

"I say two weeks tops. On another note. I'm throwing you a all white party tonight. Everyone who's anyone will be in attendance. So put on your Sundays best. Now I must be on my way. Here are the keys to the building. Around the clock, we have armed security on the post. Plus I have a state of the art camera system hooked up at all times just in case someone slips pass the security. I love you brother, but I have to go. I will text you the info on the party tonight. See you later. And young man you are a lucky guy to have someone like my brother school you to the game of life." She said while making her exit, and waving them both off.

Once the door closed behind her was when Elihu asked David to take him to one other address. He locked the doors up and activated the security system just as the first crew of security guards pulled up. He nodded at them then climbed in the back seat. Without saying a single word as David pulled away.

✗✗✗✗✗

Agent Coleman couldn't believe that she was once again assigned to an undercover case. Only this time she wasn't trying to bring down the person she was assigned to unless he does something illegal and forces her hand. Her crew comprised two other field agents. The Feds had them setup in three luxury condos being that the three of them couldn't live in one place. Each of them was issued $10,000.00 to buy clothes, shoes, bags, and cell phones. They each were allowed to take any car they wanted out of the impound.

Agent Coleman was satisfied with the place that the Feds picked out for her to live in. If she planned on getting close to a man with as much going on as Elihu she was going to at least look like she has something going on. The staged Realtor company that they gave her to run wasn't good enough for her, but it will have to do being that things were so last minute.

After showering she stood in the full body mirror and stared at her soft but toned body. She tries her best to stay fit, and eat right. She never knew when she might have to chase someone or even fight off someone that might be trying to kill her. In her line of work, there was no getting away with slacking off. If she didn't look as good as she does she wouldn't be offered the type of jobs that the Feds offer her. No drug dealer wants a chick that's only a whopper away from being fat.

Laying across the bed was the dress that she brought for tonight. It was all white and see-through, but it covered all of her private parts. The dress was made to hug every curve of her 5'4, 158 pounds frame. Her high yellow complexion, round bubble booty, and her C-cup breast always drew men to her. Unlike most women, her mom never put a perm on her hair. Her natural hair went straight down her back and stopped at the small of her buttocks. Whenever she put conditioner on her hair it curls up and looks wavy.

Plopping down on the bed with the towel wrapped around her naked body, she picked up her fake Drivers license. "Charlene Robinson!" She read it out loud. Shaking her head as if they could have picked a better name for her. Sitting the license back down she realized that the name didn't make her. She can make the name a household name.

The sound of her ringing cell phone almost made her jump out of her skin. For a moment she had forgotten that she even had a work phone. She let it ring a few times before she picked it up. "Hello, Charlene speaking."

"Hey, girl. You ready for the party tonight? Word is that there will be some major players there. Checking out a few flyers, some of Elihu's NFL bodies will show up tonight. Girl I'll quit working if I snatch one of those NFL players."

Agent Coleman pulled the phone away from her ear with a frown on her face. She knew from the moment that she laid eyes on Agent Shipment that she had some wild ways about herself. In the office, she did her best to cover it up but being a woman from the hood herself, she could spot a ratchet chick anywhere. Not wanting to make her feel like a whore or gold digger so she just played along with her as if she was looking for the same thing. "I hear you girl. I saw your dress. You going to put a hurting on everyone at the party tonight." She couldn't believe that she even fed into that. She was raised to be very ladylike by her mother, grandmother, and great aunt's. She believes that real men only want real women. The easy chicks make things hard on the strong-minded women.

After chopping it up with her for a few minutes, she cut the conversation short. "Alexa play Keyshia Cole – woman to woman!" As the song played she closed her eyes and rubbed lotion all over her smooth body. She found herself thinking of Elihu and the man she figured that he was. To say she wasn't excited about meeting him would be a lie. Standing up and looking down at her fitted white Chanel dress laying across the bed. It was different for her. Provocative, sexy, but it didn't expose too much of her body. She wanted to stand out from all the women she knew would show up half naked trying to get the men attention. If she knew Elihu character like she thought she did her dress would draw him straight to her. The hairdresser slayed her natural long and silky hair. Her eyebrows were done, and she didn't need much makeup. Checking the time on her diamond in crushed Cartier watch. The all white party is due to start in another 45 minutes, so she started getting dressed.

CHAPTER FIVE

Tonight was the night that anybody who was anybody wanted to show their face. No one didn't want to miss the chance to run into or get to meet the legendary Elihu Israel. He hadn't been home a full week and already he had been giving back to the hoods of Dade County. Off-duty City of Miami and Metro-Dade cops were patrolling the party. No guns were allowed in the party tonight, and if you didn't have a ticket you were not getting in.

Standing at the door were three of Elihu Israelite brothers dressed in white. They even had their dreads covered up. People that could not get inside settled with taking pictures with the Israelites standing at the door. No dime was spared just to make this night perfect. Elihu had no doubt that the Feds and many other agencies will be in the building tonight. He welcomed them. He wanted the world to see greatness in the making.

Unlike most, Elihu is the first person to show up to his event. As people made their way inside he greeted everyone with a handshake and a hug. He wanted to teach others about a real brotherhood. The knowledge that he has to share with his brothers and sisters stretches far and wide.

Once the party got crowded he started making rounds getting to know everyone that came out to support him. While having a conversation with three young ladies about Child support, giving them reasons why he feels like women should not put their kid's fathers on it he spotted a seductive looking woman pass by with hair that fell down her back. Not trying to be rude but his eyes followed her for a moment. Before excusing himself from the three young ladies he mentioned to them he's going to further speak on the issue. They just giggled noticing the woman that caught his eyes.

Making his way through the crowd he ended up losing her because of so many people grabbing hold of him. Turning back around searching for her for the last time he ran right into the woman that used to hold the key to his heart. She was just as beautiful as she was when they were a lot younger. Standing beside her was her husband Jeff with a smile on his face. 15 years had passed forcing him to get over her. Not once had he ever wanted the worst for her. To be honest with himself he prayed that she will have happiness even if it is not with him. He could not blame her for leaving him. While she was home pregnant with their twins, he was out living recklessly with a white woman who name he did not know. Then the accident that took three people lives. The media did not make things better for him either. For many nights he just wanted to tell her he was sorry. Unconsciously the word "sorry" slipped out of his mouth.

Lisa could not take the sight of seeing him. She thought she could manage. Just the word Sorry brought so much pain back. With tears flowing down her face she walked away from him.

He wanted to grab hold of her and console her but that was no longer his job. She washed her hands with him many years ago. He couldn't fault her for hating him, but he figured that she'll be over it by now. Seeing for himself that she still couldn't bear to see his face, he just thought that they may never be social again.

Turning towards the stage as Kimberly tapped on the Mic trying to get everyone attention he spotted the beautiful specimen of a woman standing off in the corner looking dead at him. She gave him a warm smile then focused her attention on the stage. She was making a jester with her head for him to go up on stage. So caught up in her trance for a moment he didn't even hear Kimberly calling for him to come up to the stage.

"Elihu come on up. Everyone here came to see you." Kimberly announced while waving for him to join her on the stage. Smiling while showing off her pearly white teeth with a little giggle. She was so full of life.

With all the attention on him now he had no choice but to head up to the stage. He figured that he'll make time for her once he comes down from the stage. Walking up to Kimberly he waved at the crowd.

"Thanks, sister. And wow I really appreciate you all for coming out. I'm not going to bore you all tonight so I'm going to just get straight to the point. Can I get all the ladies in the building to make their way to the front?" The room shifted as the men took a few steps back while the women made their way towards the stage.

"Good evening ladies. You special beings are the reason the American government is so rich. You ladies are also the same reason the prison system is overpopulated. I know you all are asking yourself how are you responsible for imprisoning your own husbands and boyfriends. The answer is child support and government assistance. Ladies for everything that the government gives you, they're taking two things away from you. Back in the 50's and 60's black families used to work things out by themselves, and stick by each other's side. The white man brought confusing into the black homes by closing down the factories that helped provide for our families and brought drugs into the picture. They even opened tons of liquor stores and check cashing stores in the hood. Knowing that we would one day stop by and get a drink. That one drink turns into two drinks and before we knew it we couldn't make it through our day without drinking. They trapped us. For the women that were constantly being abused by their drunk husbands or baby daddies had finally had enough. They accepted that Hud housing, or Section 8 voucher. Now by accepting that the woman had to give up information about her husband or kids father. With Hud housing, the woman doesn't have to pay any rent or reduced rent due to her income. The downside to this no one is allowed to live under the roof with a felony charge of any kind. So let's just say that her oldest son goes out and commit a robbery. Now he has to get taken off the lease or she loses her place when the rent office finds out that her son is living under the roof she can lose her place." He gave them a minute to think about everything that he just said to them before he continued.

"Now with child support. Women if you dating a man and he's not working. Don't lay down and have a child with him unless you're willing to provide for this child on your own. Because you both knew that he wasn't working or even had a way to provide for the child. Now the child turns 3 years old and daycare is killing you. You need money from your baby daddy and he still doesn't have a dollar. Now you feel that you have no choice but to comply with child support because he gave you no other option. By him having no money. The government suspends his driver's license. They continue to bill him, and he never pays. Now they lock him up for either putting his hands on you or for failing to comply with child support. Now he has a felony on his record. His chances of getting a good paying job are out of the window. The point I'm trying to make is that we don't need the government to interfere with our lives. If we stop complaining about our lives and start doing something about it ourselves we will continue to be beneath the whites. If you people will just take a chance with me we all can make a change. I'm going to open more businesses and hire more felons. We're going to build more affordable homes for us. To make this happen it will take each and every one of us." Everyone in the room was hanging on to every word that he said. He figured that he'll give them more being that they wanted to hear more.

Agent Coleman had to agree with every word Elihu had to say tonight. Bringing up child support and government assistance was the best place to start his speech. The government makes millions of dollars off of women living off welfare. It's the least the government can do for blacks being that they are making billions of taxed dollars off prisons. By her working law enforcement, she has the chance to see first hand how the government plays blacks against blacks. For every white male imprisoned fifteen or more blacks are locked behind cages.

Once Elihu concluded his speech she made her way towards him. Before he went up on stage she noticed that he had been following her. She was different unlike the women he was so used to chasing behind him. With a smile on her face, she held her hand out to shake his. "That was a very touching speech you gave. I can only wish that more women could've heard you speak those words." She noticed that he had a nice firm grip, but he was compassionate at the same time.

"Glad to know that you enjoyed it, but you are? I never saw you around." There was something about her he couldn't place. His gut told him she was there for other reasons than everyone else in the building.

"Charlene. Charlene Robinson." She replied while noticing that he was still holding onto her hand.

"Charlene Robinson. That name doesn't ring a bell. So what brings you to my all white party?" He finally released her hand realizing that it might make her feel uncomfortable. Looking deep into her dreamy eyes he found himself taken in her beauty. She had to be the most gorgeous women in the party.

"I heard about you through a friend of a friend. So I figured that I'll come out and see what all the fuss is about myself. I must say that I'm glad that I came. Your words. Your words can move mountains. You knew just how to say all the right things to the women here knowing that you were really talking to the men. My grandmother used to always say. Never listen to what someone says. Listen to what they're not saying or what they might be trying to say. Sounds like you have a way with words."

He chuckled, "You think I'm just all talk? When it comes to my fellow black people I vowed to uplift them. If I can't help someone I'll take a step back or find someone that can help."

She believed him. His demeanor said that he had no reason to lie. They found themselves finding a corner and carrying on with their conversation. They shared a few laughs and talking about some worldly things. Before he was snatched away from her they managed to exchange phone numbers.

"Looks like the two of you hit it off pretty well." Said, Agent Shipman, as she approached Agent Coleman from behind.

Agent Coleman couldn't help but notice that her partner was tipsy. Her voice slurred, and her breath smelled like Hennessy. "Nicole I really think you should consider taking an Uber home."

"No need girl. I got a hot date tonight. He's tall black and handsome. I'm going to ride his face like a cowgirl from Texas. I'll call you in the morning with details. Later girl."

Agent Coleman just shook her head as Agent Shipman left the building arm locked with a strange man. She couldn't knock her sleeping with random men just wasn't her style. She finished her drink and gave Elihu another warm smile from across the room before making her exit. She succeeded at what she came out tonight to do. As she approached the door to leave she bumped into two guys that stood out to her. They looked as if they were there for different reasons than anyone else in the party. Turning around to get a second look at them she realized that they weren't there when Elihu was speaking. Watching them closely they walked straight to Elihu and he greeted them both with a brotherly huge. Captioning the moment then she left for the night.

CHAPTER SIX

Today was the day Elihu and his two most trusted friends take the trip to Mexico. Snoop the pilate was flying the used Jet that Elihu brought a few days ago. Things are starting to look up for him. His plan was in motion. His followers were getting into position and were waiting on their first shipment.

"Snoop how much longer do we have to be on this damn plane?" Venom asked growing impatient.

"Relax my brother. We'll get there. Have a seat and allow Snoop to do what he does." Elihu poured him a glass of Patron and dropped two ice cubes in the glass.

"It's my nerves. These damn Mexicans only care about their kind. We're black. It's unheard of that they'll ever do business with a black man. What makes us so special?" Venom trusted his friend, but he didn't trust the Mexicans. "They're going to kill us and take every dollar you brought over here with us."

Elihu remained humble. He knew that everyone wasn't going to understand the things he does. He didn't feel like he had to explain his friendship with Gustavo Dominguez. "Bruh all you have to do is sit back and relax. If anything I'm the only one putting my life in danger. You can stay on the Jet while I go and handle my business, or you can straighten up while we handle business." He had to admit he'll probably be afraid also if he didn't have Gustavo in his pocket.

Once Snoop prepared them for landing Elihu pulled out the piece of paper from Gustavo. After googling the message he still didn't have a single idea what the message meant. All he knows is what Gustavo told him.

"If you ever need anything look this person up. They'll be able to help you out."

After landing in Mexico the three of them climbed in the back seat of the black on black Chevy Tahoe that awaited them on the airstrip. Elihu instructed the driver to take them to their hotel. As they road through the town, each of them looked out at the unfamiliar sights. Passing through the slums all they could smell was spicy food being cooked. Seemed like every other block they passed there was some type of restaurant or someone selling live chickens to the shoppers. No one seemed to have a car. Everyone looked to be walking everywhere they needed to go or riding on scooters.

When they reached the tourist area they found the first McDonald's, Burger King, and many more American places to eat. The driver pulled up to the front entrance of the hotel they'll be staying in for the next few days.

Elihu tipped him nicely then headed inside the hotel lobby. His friends were blown away from the layout of the hotel structure. "Fellas this is how we should live for the rest of our lives. Y'all continue to stick with me and we will have this and so much more. Now let's get settled then we can hit the streets. I brought enough money with me for us to have the time of our lives. And fellas no debit or credit cards. We don't need any paper trails that can trace us back to being in Mexico."

"Cash only it is." Said Snoop getting where Elihu was coming from.

After checking in at the front desk each of them headed to their own room. Elihu made them agree to meet back up in time to hit the strip club tonight. Just as he grabbed his room key Charlene was texting his phone. Opening the text she had sent him a picture of herself with "I hope my picture brighten up your day," Message in closed with it.

"Indeed it did." He said replying to her text. He had to admit that there was something about Her that made him want more.

They continued to go back and forward with the texting while he laid down in the bed. They were like to high school students talking over the phone. Through conversation, they were getting closer and closer to each other. He wondered if he was feeling this way because he hasn't been with another woman in 15 years. Being lonely could make him easy to fall for anyone he thought. At the same time, he feels like he should really get to know Charlene or just keep her around as someone to vibe with.

After what seemed like spending forever on the phone he decided to end the conversation for now. He needed a little rest before their night out on the town. Hanging up the phone with a smile on his face then he took another look at the picture she sent him. He figured that this picture was the first of many more to come. Closing his phone and placing it on the charger before falling asleep.

Don Royce had been sitting in front of his computer for hours. His fingers were starting to hurt from punching numbers into his calculator over and over only to come up with the wrong count. The money in his account didn't match the numbers he kept calculating on his calculator. It's been over a week since he killed Mike for messing up his money. Now here he is again with the same problem. Placing his reading glasses on the desk while he rubbed his eyes. At his old age, the walls seemed to be closing in on him. Applying pressure to business owners has been his strength for so many years, and now someone is doing the same thing to him. Apart of him wanted to listen to his wife and step down, and another part of him refused to be forced out. He is a Don, and Don's don't fold for anyone. It was time for him to make his face known again in the streets. Back in Boston he never had these types of problems until a deal went bad, and he had to relocate his family for their safety.

Pulling out the top draw of his desk. He pushed aside the couple of envelopes that were covering up a picture frame. Grabbing the frame then he placed it on the desk. In the picture stood himself, and three of his Buddies from Boston. The photo was taken after they made their first score. All four of them were dressed exactly alike in jeans, white T-shirts, and black leather jackets. On that day they battled to become the Boss of all Bosses.

"I still remember that day as if it were yesterday. The four of you had so much hunger in Y'all. It didn't take long before the Feds got involved. I can close my eyes and still see the police gunning down Wallie. Moving down here to Miami and Changing our names had to be the smartest thing that you ever came up with." She understood why they had to leave and as his wife, she vowed to never question his decision to run. She'll rather have her husband out here in the free world with her other than him being dead or in jail for the rest of his life.

He had no idea that she was even standing there behind him. "I have been thinking. You might be right. We had a good run-in the game. It might be wised to quit while I'm ahead. I just hate the fact that I feel like I'm being forced out. I have never been afraid of a good fight. Apart of me wants to die muscling people out of their money. Then that would make me selfish. I need some time to really think about this. But if I do this there won't be any more money coming in from the streets."

"Robert I could care less about this underworld. We still have our restaurants to fall back on. Just stop this now. If you don't give up this lifestyle it will be the death of you. These young kids don't have any respect for the old players. You have been sitting at this computer all morning and the numbers still haven't changed. You can't trust any of these kids. One of these days you're going to walk out of this door and never walk back through it. Chose to die of old age with me or to die in the streets leaving me widowed. The choice is yours, Don Robert." She said then left out of the room. She wasn't about to stand around and watch him make the wrong decision.

Everything that his wife said made perfect sense. The bookie business had finally become too much for him. There was no way he could run the number houses and his five-star restaurants. He had to count his blessings he had a thirty plus years run, running numbers. Most dealers his age either spent over ten years in prison or lost half their family do to someone trying to rob them.

Placing the picture and calculator back in the desk draw then he turned the computer off. A change was sure to come he just doesn't know how much will change once he pulls back. For now, he's just going to spend most of his time with his beautiful wife. He figured that whoever the corporate is that's trying to bring him down will eventually show his or her face. When the person does he'll be ready for them. He took one last look at the computer then turned the room light out.

CHAPTER SEVEN

The night was young, and the weather was just right in Mexico. Elihu and his crew were ready to get their night started. Usually, Elihu doesn't like attention to be on him but things are different for tonight. Tonight he was wearing a five-pound solid gold Cuban link necklace. The matching bracelet will also demanded the attention of whoever lays eyes on it.

Parked outside the hotel was the same driver that picked them up from the airport. Whenever he found a good thing he usually tries not to change it up. Once all three of them piled into the back of the Tahoe Elihu requested for the driver to take them to Club Pasion, club passion in English.

"Are you sure me friend? This club you is asking for is in Barranca de la Laja. It's known for Cartel activity. I don't think it will be a good idea for you Americans to step foot in that area. How about I take you three to some tourist clubs?" He was not trying to have the death of them on his hands. He knew for sure they'll be dead in minutes once he drops them off there. If they don't lose their life for being American, the jewelry that Elihu was wearing would for sure be the cause of their murder.

"listen I'm paying you to take us where I said, or do we need to find a new driver?" Elihu asked while fanning a stack of hundred dollar bills in his face.

"It's your funeral, my friend." Without another word, he put the SUV in drive heading for club Pasion.

Venom looked over at Elihu. There was no sign of fear on his face. Most people would be terrified about entering a dangerous neighborhood that they were unfamiliar with in the states. The Cartel protected towns in Mexico were the worst areas to visit if you weren't Mexican. But here they are dressed like a million bucks without a single gun on them. They would be sitting ducks for whichever Cartel gets to them first.

Once they got on the dirt road that leads up the mountain there was no turning back. When the driver came to a stop they were parked outside of the strip club. Elihu gave him a nice tip and instructed for him to wait on them. In the mountains, there were no such things as a taxi or bus. He agreed to wait no longer than 3 hours or he was gone.

Climbing out the back seat of the Tahoe everyone standing outside the club was staring at them. Paying the stares no mind as they entered the club. From the outside, the club looked like a shit hole. On the inside was a different story. Weed smoke had the club fogged up. There were four different stages scattered out with over 25 dancers performing tonight.

Elihu lead the way to a table in the back were their backs would be against the wall. If anyone had a problem he needed to see them coming. Before they could get comfortable at their table one of the bartenders was there and ready to serve them.

"Do you Americans know where you are? We never had blacks in here before. But is there anything that I can get you three to drink?"

"I guess it's a first time for everything. We'll take a bottle of Patron if you have it." Elihu had to admit her body was beautiful. For her petite size, her curves were just right.

Yes, Patron. 200.00 American dollars." She took the money out of his hand and couldn't help but noticed the large knot of cash that he was holding. From what she saw the money was all one hundred dollar bills.

He wanted her to see his pocket full of money. The money is what will bring the slum dogs his way. By the time the bartender brought back their bottle, four strippers were in their section trying to make some money. He figured that he'll give a few dollars out while trying to have an excellent time. Out of the four, he picked the shortest one with an ass like a black woman. He cashed in a thousand dollars for straight one dollar bills. Making it rain on the four strippers. By now he had everyone in the club attention.

"Papi would you like to go to the back. In back I'll fuck and suck you for $50.00." She said into his ear because the loud music was drowning everything else out.

He figured that she was offering him a steal because he would've paid top dollar for her. Nothing else needed to be said he bounced up out of his seat and allowed her to lead him to the back room. Before entering the hallway that leads to the back room stood one of the biggest Mexicans that he ever saw. After tipping him to enter the back, Elihu followed closely behind her with thoughts of how he would fold her up. She just didn't know that he got 15 years of pressure for her. Thinking to himself that he might break her in half while trying to bust a nut.

Once in the room, she closed the door behind him. Coming from the hood he knew better than to get butt ass naked. He pulled his shirt off and let his boxer shorts and pants fall to his ankles. She took one look at his thick horse looking dick and said a silent prayer because she planned on dying trying to take all of it inside of her.

After allowing her to clean off the seat he sat his bare ass down while she got on her knees in front of him than she licked the head of his dick. He tried his best to relax while she used her mouth to suck him into a full erection. She'd suck him up slowly, then she'll pick up the pace moving fast. So much slob covered his entire dick to the point her slob was running down his balls.

He didn't want to cum in her mouth, so he pulled her head back then used his teeth to rip open the gold xl condom. After wiping her slob off of his dick he rolled on the condom. He motioned for her to turn around and squat on his dick. Once he entered her pussy he knew right away he would enjoy the ride. Using his left hand to pull on her hair while wrapping his right arm around her waist. He wasn't allowing her to get away as he made her bounce all the way down on his dick. She pushed his dick out of her so she could squirt on the floor. Just as she finished squirting he was sticking his dick back inside of her.

He flipped her over never taking his dick out of her. Leaning her over on the stool while he worked her in the middle. Taking his right hand he massaged her tits while never missing a stroke. He planned to make her work for his money. When he finishes with her she will tattoo his name on her pussy. He knows that no one in the entire Mexico never fucked her the way he's fucking her right now. Feeling his nut building up he braced himself to cum. The room door burst open and two Mexicans ran inside, guns in hand, while he was filling the condom up with cum. The one on the right cracked him upside the head with the butt of his AK-47 knocking Elihu out cold. They quickly tied him up and dragged him out the back door of the club. Tossed his unconscious body into the trunk of the beat up Toyota Camry. Without a trace they speeded away before anyone can suspect any foul play.

The driver of the Tahoe figured that something had to be wrong when he noticed the three Mexicans speeding away. Turning off the truck he ran inside the nightclub to check on his passengers. They were there less than an hour and he feels like their life is in danger. When he made it in the club he spotted two of the three. Not seeing the big guy anywhere he approached the two. "Where's Elihu?"

"He went to the back room with her," Snoop shouted while pointing at the beauty that just came from the back. Without a second thought, he and Venom were jumping over the wall and headed straight for her with death in their eyes.

Her reaction was late Venom had already slapped the taste out of her mouth. Before he could get a second lick on her the club full of Mexicans stood up like they all wanted trouble. If he had his gun and some crack cocaine to smoke he'll take them all on. Right now they were outnumbered so he back away from the dancer. The exit door was blocked. The Mexicans were holding them in the club. Venom and Snoop just took a seat at the table they had been sitting in. They were stuck until everything come back clean on Elihu. If not all three of them are dead men.

✗✗✗✗✗

A cup of water to the face was what woke Elihu from his deep sleep. His hands were still tied behind his back. He was dressed in his tank top and boxer shorts. The Mexicans that snatched him in the club thoroughly checked his clothes for any sign of him being a Federal agent. All they found was a piece of notebook paper in his pocket. What was writing on the paper was the only reason he wasn't hanging upside down by his feet.

Focusing his eyes he realized that he was in a room full of Mexicans. Each of them standing there completely quiet with machetes in their hands. They all seemed to move to the side as a woman made her way to the front dressed in a white sundress. Her heels sounded off with every step she took. She stopped no more than 15 feet away from him. His eyes rose up from her feet to her face. Judging by the way the soldiers were treating her she had to be the person in charge.

"Who are you and why are you in Mexico?" She asked while taking the note that Gustavo gave to him from one of the men that kidnapped him from the club.

"My name is Elihu Israel, and I'm here looking for help. My Good friend Gustavo Dominguez told me that if I should ever need anything I should come to Mexico with that note that he personally wrote for me. I don't want any problems. I want help that's all."

"Silence!" She said cutting him off as she read the phrase that only she and Gustavo would know. The rest of the message was Gustavo explaining that Elihu was family and that he trusted him with his very own life. "Get up." She commanded him. "Cut him loose and bring him into the other room." She said out loud to no one in particular, but they all rushed to his side trying to free him from bondage.

Once he was cut loose he rushed to keep up with her. Following behind her up a flight of stairs. Once they got to the top he noticed that the layout was of a cozy home. Being that people are butchered downstairs he figured that the upstairs was a front for anyone passing by. He noticed that there wasn't a single picture of anyone in the entire house.

"Elihu have a seat. Would you like a drink?" She offered while snapping her fingers. Within seconds one of her men was offering to pour him a drink.

"I'm good right now on the drink. You have a very nice home here."

"Oh, you funny. This isn't my home. My brother Gustavo says that he trusts you with his life. Knowing my brother he's not the type to socialize with many people. So tell me about the situation he had got into while you two were in prison together?" She asked trying to get a better feel of the situation.

Elihu went on to explain everything that took place in the few years that he and Gustavo were roommates. Unknowing to him Gustavo had been grooming him for the meeting with his sister. "So you really are the leader of the Dominguez Cartel?"

"In the flesh. I must say that you are such a very special person to my family now. A brother of my brother is a brother of mine."

"Uh, where my friends though?"

"They're safe. I'm trying to figure out what you want or need from me before we meet with your friends."

"I have to admit your English is excellent. But while locked up I never asked Gustavo was he apart of any Cartel even though it was rumored. He and I were just cool with each other. It's an honor to even be sitting here having a conversation with you. Since I'm here I believe that I can help you, and we both can make a lot of money."

"How can you help me, Elihu? My business is already worth millions of dollars. What you looking for 5 or 10 kilos of Coke?"

"Now I need over 100 kilos. I have over a thousand followers and they're ready to move whatever I bring to the table."

"A hundred keys. That's a lot of cocaine for someone that never dealt in coke before. I hope you can forgive me I had my men search your room and they found a bag full of money. $5,000,000.00 in cash. Either you're straight up crazy or very brilliant. No one in their right mind would come to Mexico with this much money. You were even in the club looking like a million bucks while flashing thousands of dollars. What were you thinking? Were you trying to get killed?"

He just smirked. "To be honest everything I did was to end up right here where I am now. I figured that if I go out to the club in the slums looking like a tourist that I would draw some attention. I only wished that my actions didn't end up getting me and my friends killed. I trusted in Gustavo and the letter he gave me. I figured that whoever tried to rob me or Kidnapped me would read the letter and it would be enough to free me. And it did, and here I am sitting talking with you. My plan worked out perfectly I'll say."

Saudy had to admit Elihu plan worked to his benefit. "I like the fact that you think things through. Most people won't go as far to think of trying something that dangerous. Without that letter, you lose your life downstairs and I never know who you are or even if you're in the country." She pushes his bag of money towards him. "Not one single dollar has been removed from the bag. If you are looking for a connect you found the best one in the country. I have people in Miami that will deliver product to you whenever you need it. But there is one problem. I already have someone in the states I'm doing business with. I need him to know that he's replaceable. Take care of him and I'll open the floodgates for you."

He just shook his head. He knew that dealing with drugs he'll have to kill or have someone killed one day. He just didn't think he'll be ordering his first murder before he even receives a brick of coke. "Give me all the info needed on this person. Their days are numbered as soon as I get back to the states."

"ok, that's it for that. For the rest of the night, we're going to really get to know each other. No one must know that you have any connections to Mexico. After we do any talking over the phone destroy it. We will leave no traces that can possibly lead back to each other. To this day no one knows who's in charge of the Cartel. So I can move around freely, and I plan on keeping it that way. That's enough talk about business, let's enjoy the night." Saudy grabbed Elihu by the hand while showing him around and introducing him to everyone necessary.

The sun was coming up by the time Saudy finished prepping him to become a drug lord. Elihu, Venom, and Snoop were flying back to Miami in silence. Each of their lives was about to change once they take out their contract. Step two of his plan was already in motion. There was no backing out now.

CHAPTER EIGHT

Elihu was glad that he made it back to Miami safely but now he has work to do. Saudy threw a monkey wrench in his plans. He figured that he'll have to pay for the drugs but killing someone was not in the plans. There was no way he would let murdering one person keep him from for filling his dreams. For now, he planned on spending a whole day with his kids. He sent David to go and pick them up from their mom house. Hearing the alarm system beeping he figured that could only be his twins. After freshen up he headed down the stairs to start their day off with breakfast.

"Kids good morning. Welcome to my home. Of course, you both can have any room in the house you'll like. Before you pick out your rooms my chef prepared us some breakfast."

"This is a nice crib you got here dad. How many beds and bathrooms you got?" Eric asked looking over the plush living room. He figured that his dad didn't spare a single dollar for his home.

"10 bedrooms and 6 full bathrooms. I got this house for the two of you also. You both are welcomed to stay here as long as you both shall want."

"This place is nice dad, but you know we're staying with mom. By the way, she asked me to have you call her." Erica wasn't trying to hurt his feelings for moving in with him because he was trying to build a bond with them.

David figured that he'll excuse himself. This conversation didn't include him, so he made his exit.

Elihu just stood there and looked at his kids for a second. His son Eric looked exactly like him when he was his age. Erica put him in the mind of his sister Kimberly, with Lisa complexion. He was grateful that his kids were allowing him to be a part of their lives even though he missed their entire lives. The only thing there was left for him to do is just be their father. The twins are 14 years old. Freshmen in high school. It was too late to baby them. The only thing left to do was give them the real world.

“Ok. No more of me trying to baby you guys. In the next four years, you both will be grown and out of me and your mom house. I will give you both two hundred and fifty thousand dollars. The only catch is that you must turn the money over. That's more than enough money for you both to create your own businesses doing whatever you like. I might be your dad and have a lot of money but you two are my kids and you'll have to earn every dollar you get from me. I need Y'all to always remember that nothing in life is free. Now come on and let's eat before the food gets cold.” Elihu said while wrapping an arm around both kids neck and walking them into the dining room area.

“Yea Pops I can really make something happen with that type of money. How long before you kick out the bread?” Eric asked while taking his seat at the table.

“Yea Dad that type of money will give us a head start at paving our own future. I really appreciate that.” Erica had to admit she was starting to love the fact that her father is around now.

“I'll have the money separated between you both by the end of the week. This money is to only be spent on things that generate money. We just never know how life may turn out so you both must do the right thing. I may not have been around Y'all throughout y'all whole life but you both have my genes. In some type of way, you both should have my ways.” He couldn't stop staring at his kids. He could see that they're some good kids. Since the first day, they met each other all three of them were giving each other a chance to be a part of each other's lives.

Sitting at the table for what seemed like hours as they told jokes about their past and just talked about things that they may have never known about each other. Elihu was glad that his kids were giving him a chance to be a father to them both.

After leaving the dining room they took their conversation into the living room. Elihu just sat there with a smile on his face as the kids caught him up on everything that they could remember from their past. He figured that he could listen to them talk for the rest of the day. There was so much that he didn't know about his kids. He wanted to be mad at Lisa for keeping them away from him for so long. Publicly cheating on Lisa was too much for her to bare, plus the car crash. He ruined everything that they were supposed to be.

His ringing cell phone interrupted their bonding time. Noticing that Venom was the caller he excused himself for a moment. Stepping back into the kitchen as he picked up the call. "What's good bruh? What have you learned?"

"Everything. Me and Snoop are at the front gate. Buzz us in."

Elihu pushed the remote for the front gate on his cell phone as he hung up and headed for the front door. By the time he unlocked the door Venom and Snoop were parking behind his Bentley truck. He had them both clean up their appearance because he couldn't have his kids seeing them looking like crack heads. They both had their dreads pulled back into a ponytail and they trimmed up the edge of their hairline.

"Good morning fellas. Come right on in. Once I introduce you both to my kids, then we'll take our conversation to my office." He made sure to give them both a brotherly hug then closed the door behind them.

After introducing them both to his kids he gave both kids a knot of money and told them to go shopping on him. Once he instructed David to take the kids any place they wanted to go the three of them made their way into his office to handle grown folks business.

Once the door was closed did Elihu take a seat behind his desk. "What did y'all find out about this person?"

"He's a spokesman that's running for Mayor in the up incoming election. Word on the streets is that he has the best chance to win. What we also learned is that he has been shaking down everyone that he knows is dipping their hand in a cookie jar just to make ends meet. He's a real slime ball." Venom reported while handing Elihu the envelope of information.

"He also got a crew of young gunners out of Liberty City and Carol City that's pushing his drugs. In return, he keeps the police off of them. These kids are reckless. They move throughout the streets as if they're untouchable. Inclosed you'll also find pictures of each crew leader. Addresses to all the properties they live in on down to the cars they drive. All you have to do now is tell us when you would like for us to make a move on them?" Snoop asked after sharing the information that he found.

Elihu was pleased with everything that they found out in just one night. He'll hate to end up on the other end of Venom & Snoop's gun. They both were army trained. They both specialized in any type of firearm. They both were kicked out of the armed forces because of drug addiction. Crack cocaine brought them both down. Before being sent home Venom shot a friendly in the back. For that, he was shipped off to Federal prison where he was diagnosed as crazy, so he only had to spend 7 years behind bars. The two of them on the city streets together was never a good thing. They tend to get excited when someone shoots back at them.

"I'm going to let you two run loose. We're going to start from the bottom and work our way up. I wanna take food off of Mr. Pete Wilson table and watch him scrambled to pick up the pieces. A man with his status probably believes that no one is brave enough to fuck with his money. There's a new Boss in town and I don't want him to find out about us until its time to snatch the city from underneath his feet. Can Y'all handle this?"

"Can we handle it. Shit, this is what we live for. You handle the business side of things while we take out everyone that try to stand in your way." For Venom the next best thing to getting high was taking someone life.

CHAPTER NINE

After days of flirting with each other Elihu decided to ask Charlene out on a date. He figured that they could start their night with a delicious dinner. Not knowing exactly where to take her so he asked his sister Kimberly. She explained to him that Italian Pot was the place to take a date to eat.

Once David pulled in front of the restaurant Elihu climbed from out the backseat then rushed around the Bentley truck and held the back door open for his beautiful date. Looking at her in the moonlight the stars seemed to compliment her flawless skin. The Chanel evening dress that he brought for her called for everyone's attention. Taking her soft and smooth hand in his as he helped her out of the backseat. Hands down they were the best looking couple there tonight. The cameraman just fell in love with them and went to snapping pictures. At that very moment, Elihu realized that he wanted her to be around. Not only was she beautiful but she had brains and she shared his love and passion for helping black people.

After checking on his reservation they were escorted to their table. Sitting on the table was a dozen fresh cut roses and a bottle of Rose. He took the opportunity to pull her chair out for her once she took her seat he helped her scoot under the table.

"Thank you." She gratefully said to him. "This place is nice." She took a moment just to take in the beautiful restaurant. Along the walls were pictures of different movie stars playing mob bosses and there were even a few real mob bosses on the wall. The smell of tomato sauce was in the air. The restaurant had a very chill vibe. She could tell that they catered to the rich and the famous.

"Yes, it is. You eat Italian right?" He asked while chuckling knowing that it was a little too late to be asking that question.

"Yes, I love Italian food. Italian is one of my favorite foods to eat after soul food. Lord knows that I love some bbq ribs, greens, and mac & cheese. After every Thanksgiving, I have to run 4 miles three days out of the week for 3 months just to keep this figure of mine right."

"You have been doing a great job because you look damn good to me. But why don't you have any kids? Did you have any abortions, or you just don't like kids?" The fact that she doesn't have any kids been killing him. Someone as breathtaking as her should have four kids he thought.

She rested her chin in the palm of her hand as she looked at him. The questions he asks always seem to come out of nowhere she thought. "No abortions, plus I never tried to have any kids either. I guess I never ran into that special someone that I would love to have a child for. Honestly, I feel like having kids by the wrong person things will turn out toxic. Having kids with the real love of your life guarantees that you will grow old with the love of your life. I still believe in that fairytale love. Beauty & the Beast. When I fall in love with my Beast I'm going to open myself to him and give him all the kids that I can have."

Reading the sparkle in her eyes he knew that he was the Beast she was referring to. She was definitely the beauty that he had been searching for. "Wow, that was deep. I'm grateful for all the fuck ups that came before me." He said to her while holding up his glass of water.

"Good evening I'll be you guys server for tonight? Here's the menu. I'll give you a few minutes to look it over before I come back." Before running off to see about her other tables she told them her name.

Neither of them expected for a black woman to be working in the elegant restaurant. Charlene looked around trying to see if the young lady was helping any white people. Noticing her as she bounced around the restaurant helping multiple different people did she turn around and sat straight in her chair.

The couple that entered the restaurant and was receiving all type of love from the diners caught his eyes. They were a lot older than he remembered them to be. He never took his eyes off of them until they entered the kitchen area. "Excuse me for a second beautiful." Without waiting for a reply he was out of his seat and heading straight for the kitchen. No one stopped him as he busted straight through the swinging doors. He looked in both directions searching for them. Looking to the right he noticed a wood door with the sign management on it. Unable to locate them any place else so he made his way to the management door. Before knocking on the door he took a deep breath. Apart of him wanted to leave and to never return but the other part of him kept saying man up.

As the door open he took two steps back. Standing behind the door was an older Italian woman with salt & pepper hair. The look on both of their faces said that they both remember. A single tear ran down the right side of her face. He knows that this might be hard on her because it's also hard on him.

"Who's at the door, honey?" Her husband asked as he stood up and approached the door. Who he found standing outside his door was the last person he ever wanted to see unless he was in a grave.

"I don't want any problems I just want to formally apologize for what I did to the two of you. I know that my words will never make things right with what I did. I wish that I could go back to that day and change my childish ways. Me not thinking cost me 15 years in prison and memories that I will never forget. So once again I'm sorry for ripping away part of your family." He said what he had to say then started walking away feeling a lot better about himself. He could care less about their forgiveness getting that off his chest was the most important thing to him.

She cleared her throat then the words came out, "Wait!" With just one look inside his eyes, she was able to see the hurt inside of him. He had served his time for his wrongdoing. She could hate him all that she wants but that would never change a thing.

Elihu stopped in his tracks but never turned around to face them again. Over time he realized that in life you can't be there to protect your family from all harm and danger. People have to be accountable for their own actions.

"I forgive you." She squeezed her husband hand while giving him a warm smile. "We forgive you."

"Thanks!" He replied then headed back to his table. Pushing open the swing kitchen door that opened up to the dining area only to run into a well-dressed brother dressed in a three-piece suit. "Excuse me."

The gentlemen face instantly turned into a frown. He was ready to go off on whoever ran into him. Until he laid eyes on the mac-truck of a man that ran into him he was forced to humble himself. "You damn near knocked me down. Gotta watch where you going, big fella."

"I could say the same thing for you, but I'll let you have that. Now if you can excuse me my date is waiting for me." Elihu stepped around him as he headed for his table.

"I know you. You're Elihu Israel. You were going to be the best player to ever play the game of football. Boy, you fucked your life up getting some head while driving. I bet you'll never do that shit again." He laughed for a moment knowing that he was getting under Elihu skin. He didn't care because he was a natural ass-hole. All he does is kick people while they're down for amusement.

"You running for Mayor right?" Elihu asked already knowing the answer to his own question.

"Yes I am, and I'm going to clean up this city. The people of Dade County needs someone like me leading them. Make sure to vote for me Pete Wilson."

"Yea I'll keep that in mind," Elihu said chomping him off while heading back to his seat.

Pete shot Elihu daggers with his eyes. For some strange reason, he couldn't help but feel like Elihu was a threat. He quickly brushed the thought off. There was no way someone could be a threat to him when they ran in separate lanes. Not once did he take his eyes off of Elihu until he took his seat at the table with a beautiful young lady. He had to admit that Elihu had this thing about himself that sparked Pete attention. He decided to lay off Elihu for now and get back to the matter at hand. He made his way inside the kitchen.

"Is everything alright. That guy just crashed right into you. I have to admit he lost his footing when he ran into you. He probably thought he ran into a brick wall." She said while lightly laughing causing Elihu to break a smile. Just a second ago he was highly upset. Thanks to her he was In a good mood again. She loved the fact that she could tame the beast. Elihu was very gentle with her but judging by the look he gave the man that ran into him there was a dark side to him. Apart of her wondered if she'll ever get to see him snap. The thought of him going beast mode on someone kind of turned her on.

"Maybe next time he'll pay more attention to where he's going for now on," Elihu said while flexing his chest. Causing his chest to bounce up and down. He loved her beautiful full smile. The more he's around her the more he wants to keep her around. He made a mental note to himself to win her heart.

By the time the waitress came, they were in a deep conversation just enjoying each other time. They quickly placed their order and ran the waitress off. Elihu wanted to get back to the story she was telling him about her life. Even after the waitress brought their food back she was still telling him stories about herself. There was something about him that allowed her to relax and be herself around him. While enjoying their food and conversation he toned everyone else out trying not to miss a thing she had to say.

After enjoying the delicious dinner he paid the tab and left a healthy tip. Once he pulled out her seat he held out his hand motioning for her to grab hold of his. Treating her like a real gentleman should as he escorted her outside. The valet driver had his car pulled up front. David was behind the wheel awaiting his orders.

"Let's go home, David!" Elihu stated while staring in her eyes. She never let on like she didn't want to go home with him. As they pulled away from the restaurant they just cuddled with each other. They both were locked into their own thoughts.

Charlene was in complete aw once David pulled inside the white bar gate. The yard looked to be freshly manicured, with colorful flowers in different sections of the gardens. The two-story house that was made of mostly glass made her jaw drop. She figured that people with money would have nice houses, but she didn't think Elihu would be living in such a house. Stepping out of the back seat, the first thing she noticed was the number of cameras he had securing the house.

Placing her hand in his as David drove away in the truck. She allowed Elihu to lead her into the house. Once in the door, she didn't know if she should take her heels off or keep them on. The white tile floor was so clean you could eat off of it. Looking at the man Elihu was she figures that he must have a team of maids to clean up his house.

Elihu stood there and watched her take in the sights of his home. "Would you like a tour of the place?" He asked with his back pressed against the door as he enjoyed the view that stood before his eyes. She had to be the most beautiful woman that he ever laid eyes on. He loved the way her fat ass poked out in her fitted dress.

Feeling his stare she turned around to face him only to find him leaning against the door. The bulge in his pants was like a hint of what he really wants to show her. It's been quite a while since she had any herself and tonight she wasn't about to play hard to get.

"Ah, Charlene I can't lie. I'm feeling you, and I'll like for the two of us to get a lil closer if that's alright with you?" He felt like a chump once he thought about his choice of words. Whenever he was around her his choice of words never seem to flow the way he would usually say them.

She shyly put her head down like a little girl then said, "Yes I'll be your girlfriend if that's what you are asking me?" in the back of her mind she couldn't help but feel like she was wrong. She was the FBI and he was not a suspect of any crime. "*Why should it be a crime if I give him some?*" She asked herself while stepping closer to him.

"I got a thing for you and I want you to be my girl. Let me be the man in your life. I know there may be many others trying to win your heart, but I promise to lead you in the right direction. I promise to never break your heart-"

"Don't promise me that. You never know what life has in stored for us or you. But yes I'll be your woman. Shit, I already felt like the woman of your life." She was now standing directly in front of him. Using her left hand she grabbed a handful of his dick. "Now come on and show me what this dick do?"

Elihu grabbed her so quickly catching her completely off guard then embracing her with a kiss. They kissed and kissed like two love bugs that haven't seen each other in years. Breaking their kiss he scooped her off of her feet then carried her inside the master bedroom. Clapping his hands together three times and a tint covered up the wall/ Window giving them some privacy. They could see out, but no one could see in. It gave off the allusion that someone might be watching them.

The fact that there was a chance that someone could possibly see them turned her on even more. She unzipped the back of her dress then wiggled out of it until it hit the floor. Feeling very sexy and her black silk thong.

He figured that she would be just as sexy outside of her clothes as she is when she has clothes on. Under the dim room light, he took in all of her beauty. Standing chest to breast he took his right hand and ran it down her back. Once he got to her round butt he squeezed her ass cheek real firmly. "I swear you are so beautiful." He told her while staring into her dreamy eyes.

"Thank you and you are very handsome yourself." She honestly felt like they would make a good couple together. Right now she didn't want to talk. She wanted to be punished. After placing her hand over his mouth she helped him undress. Once he had his pants and shoes off she kneeled down and pulled his boxer briefs completely off. The blood was rushing into his dick causing it to throb and bounce up and down. Just the sight of his monster dick caused her mouth to water up. She placed the head of his dick in her mouth and softly sucked on it.

She started sucking him up with love. The way she worked her mouth back and forward on his dick was as if he was her king, and she was the queen. She found herself sucking his dick as if he was in the army and was being shipped overseas in the morning and she needed him to remember what her head game was like.

Elihu had to admit he didn't expect her to perform oral sex as well as she does. Not wanting to cum in her mouth he had to pull her head away. Scooping her up from under her arms then he laid her down on the bed. Once He placed her in the position that he wanted her in on her back did he take another good look at her banging body. The thought of them sharing a life together crossed his mind and all it did was make him smile. Him being in love with her was an understatement.

Using his smooth hands and lips as he worked his way from her neck to her pussy. Her love box was cleaned shaved just the way he liked. Before performing oral he said a silent prayer that she enjoys his head game than he dug in. Using his lips and tongue as he did his best to drive her into ecstasy. The way she moaned and ran her hands through his thick dreads he figured that he had to be doing something right.

Inwardly she wanted to cry. He was putting a hurting on her love box and a good way. Unconsciously she found herself working her hip throwing her pussy in his face. Causing his nose to rub across her clit every so often.

"Yes just like that. Ohhh, please don't stop. I'm going to cum." She was working her hips even faster now working up her orgasm. Relaxing her body as she allowed her juices to flow. She came so hard for a moment she was paralyzed. As she was coming back to her senses Elihu was positioning himself between her smooth legs preparing to become one with her body for the first time. "*Oh my God, he's huge!*" She said to herself while taking in every inch of his love muscle.

After slowly easing in and out of her a few times while he starred into her dreamy eyes. He planned to enjoy every minute or second inside of her. After balancing himself upright on his arms did he slowly pick up the pace. Together they mound and grinded as their bodies seemed to become one. As their bodies heated up so did the room seemed like as the room instantly heated up. What seemed like all night they were locked on to each other lovemaking. By the time they were done they both were completely out of breath and couldn't take anymore.

CHAPTER TEN

Today was like any other day behind the prison wall. At 8:30 am the yard was open for the whole compound. Standing outside of Gustavo prison cell stood no less than fifteen Mexicans that were willing to lay their lives on the line for him. He was a made man and his crew of Mexicans made sure that everyone understood it.

Once Gustavo was ready to head out onto the Rec yard he and his crew made their way out the door. No one didn't want any parts of the deadly Cartel. Everything about Gustavo screamed made man from the way he walked, slow and at his own pace like he didn't have a care in the world. He stood at 5'4 but his presence seemed to make him a lot taller. He couldn't weigh any over 145 lbs. soaking wet. His hair was long and curly, every chance he get he like to apply jell to it just to smooth his hair out. After spending over 10 years in prison so far he doesn't have any more room for tattoos unless he will tat his face, which was something he refused to do.

Once on the Rec yard, he headed straight for his regular section only to find two Puerto Rican Blood gang members sitting there. Gustavo gave the head of his security detail one look without hesitation he sprung into action.

"Yo are you two lost?" Gustavo number two man asked the seemed to be lost gang members.

The look that the gang members shot them said that they wanted to challenge the Mexicans, but they were outnumbered so they stepped for now. Gustavo motioned for his crew to let them be. He figured that it was too early in the morning to take someone life. He just wanted to enjoy the morning breeze and feed the birds. After taking his seat it seemed like only moments later inmates starting rushing his area trying to buy drugs. It was nothing for him to get pounds of weed into the prison. The money was good, but he knew that he'll be able to make a lot more money if he could get cocaine in. His pipeline to Mexico was cut short because he didn't trust a soul. He had fate in Elihu, but he had no idea if he'll even take the trip to Mexico. He chose Elihu because he was unlike any other black man that he knew. Most blacks were greedy and would steal $10.00 out of their mom's purse. Knowing that how could he trust them with 100's or 1,000's of kilos. From the first moment, he met Elihu he knew that he was different. All of the blacks and the cell were trying to get close to him. Not once did Elihu join a gang or even cliqued up for protection. He held his on and fraught every issue that came his way on his own. When they were in the room alone all he did was read different types of books to further educate himself.

After watching him closely for over a few months Gustavo was sure that Elihu was not a federal agent. No matter how much the word spread over the compound about Gustavo affiliation to the Dominguez Cartel not once did Elihu asked him about it. It was like it didn't even matter to him. It was Gustavo turn to get to know Elihu. After another month of vibing, they were becoming cool with each other. As time continued to pass them both by they became a lot like brothers. At night when the cell doors were locked was when Gustavo would take the time out to teach Elihu a few words of Spanish. By the time Elihu was getting released from prison, he could comprehend what someone was saying to him in Spanish and somewhat speak the language. Still, he could not read or write Spanish.

He missed his black brother but he'll rather Elihu be a free man than for him to spend one more hour behind bars. Looking out over the Rec yard at all the different types of people he couldn't spot a soul that could come close to reminding him of Elihu.

"Inmate Dominguez I need to speak to you for a moment!" The female guard asked as she stood no more than 10 feet away.

He instantly recognized her as one of Elihu followers. "Do you have some news for me or something?" He asked while standing up from his seat. Waving his hand to have his men stand down. Their job was to protect him no matter the cost. They'll kill an officer as quick as a inmate. Taking life was nothing to them.

She had to admit that she was a little shaking up about being in the presence of the crazy Mexicans. "I have a gift for you from Elihu. He sends his love and is awaiting your call." With that said she handed him the cellphone and walked off.

Instantly the phone was vibrating in the palm of his hands. Answering the call while pacing the phone on speaker. "Hello!"

"Gustavo my friend. I pray that all is well with you. Plus I told you I'll never forget about you."

He was lost for words. No one has never done anything for him. The amount of people that served time with him and got released. Not one has ever looked back for him. Now here's a black man that was showing him more love than anyone in his Cartel. "E my boy. Is this line safe?"

"Safe as it will get. There's a number saved in the phone for Mexico if you know what I mean. I suggest that you remove the number from the phone."

"So you made the trip?" Gustavo still couldn't believe his eyes and ears. After only a moment he realized that he was still in prison. "Im going to have to call you back. Im still on the Rec yard right now."

"Call me whenever. But make sure you call that number in the phone today. We have so much to catch up on so don't take to long to call me back." Elihu could tell that he made Gustavo day with the cell phone. Now he could make private calls to whoever he wants in the world.

"oh I will call you tonight. Stay by the phone my brother." Gustavo hung up the call then stuffed the phone into his pockets. With a cellphone, a lot of things were about to change. There's just so much more than he could get done now.

For the rest of the morning he just sat back and watched the flow of people on the Rec yard, and all the money they were bringing his way. Life has just gotten a little bit better for him. All he could think about was the new wave was about to flood the prison. Plus all the profits will be his.

Lincoln Field was one of Miami most dangers apartments in Liberty City. If you ain't from the apartments you ain't have no business hanging out there. The city of Miami Police even have a hard time cleaning up the place because of so many different ways the drug dealers, Robbers, and killers have to escape without being apprehended. Different drug dealers claimed to be in control of the apartments, only to either get killed off by another dealer that wanted total control of the high drug activities area.

Nowadays the Bloods out of Miami Gardens have the apartments on smash. Red bandanas hung from each corner of the apartments marking their territory. Rival Blood gang members stayed far away as possible from Lincoln Field. Everyone knew that Foe was quick on the draw and had no problem killing anyone no matter the time or day. His team of young and wild gang members will lay their lives on the line for him. As the boss, he pays them well and they were terribly afraid to go against him. The last person that felt that he could challenge Foe only ended up on a T-shirt. Foe even killed his victim brothers for wearing a RIP shirt with the victim picture on it. He was just flat out crazy.

Foe usually hung out in the apartments for a couple of hours a day only trying to get a feel of what type of day his trap will have. Watching all movements with a close eye as he talked on the phone with his boss man.

"My nigga you tough for the bitches." Foe said into the phone while nodding at the young Blood that walked pass him.

"Nah next time I got you homie. Matter of fact I will set some shit up for you this weekend when we all link up. So my nigga bring your rubbers because the bitches will be there-" the person on the other end of the phone paused for a moment without asking to be excused.

No matter how tough Foe was he knew better than to hang the phone up or be stupid enough to even interrupt his boss. There was no way he would let his boss disrespect stop him from eating. They are working with the best cocaine around. Foe getting money with dealers way from Tallahassee that's copping weight. His pockets was heavy and the man on the other end of the phone was responsible for it.

"Yea what was I saying?" He asked, but he was talking more to himself. "Nigga just be there Saturday. It will be a movie."

"I'm there my boy." Foe wouldn't miss anything he had to offer for the world.

"Alright, I'm out. So fuck with me later." He said into the phone then hung up before Foe could respond.

Foe could only shake his head as he placed his iPhone 8 into his pocket. Stretching his arms while yawning he looked around his kingdom as he liked to call it. Noticing a crap game taking place on the corner he decided to make his way over to it. Shooting dice was another thing he was good at, plus he had been feeling lucky lately.

"Point seen money lost Y'all, boys. Drop what Y'all going to put down." Said the young street hustler as he shook the dice up in his hand motioning like he was ready to let the dice fly.

Foe recognized him from the apartments. He couldn't be any older than 16 years of age, but from what he had been hearing about the kid was that he is a bull with the pistol. "Young Blood I'm down like this."

"All money good. My bag longer than train smoke." The kid knew just who Foe was, but his rep didn't mean a thing to him. Plus the set of twin '40s that rested up under his t-shirt would surely rock anyone to sleep if they try him in any kind of way.

Foe had to admit he liked the kid style. Most dudes from the area could barely look him in the eye's let alone talk to him crazy. After deciding to brush the kid comments off as he stood back and watched him shoot the dice.

The two green dice stopped on a pair of two's while the red one continued to spin. Everyone who had money on the line was hoping that the dice land on a '1. Out of everyone Foe seemed like he was the only person that wasn't fazed by whatever the point might be. After the dice spun for a second or two it finally rolled over with the number 6 pointing up.

"Point seen money lost y'all boyz." The kid let them know while quickly scooping up everyone's money. When he got to Foe pile of cash he hoped that he didn't have to take things to pistol play about his bread. To his surprised Foe moved his feet out of the way. "I appreciate it, fellas. Who getting back down?"

A couple of petty dealers dropped a couple more stacks of money on the ground with hopes of winning some of their money back. Foe on the other hand figured that either the kid had a hot hand or some hot dice. Meaning the dice was loaded to land only on a 6. Today he had no attention on killing anyone, so he decided to let the kid have the couple of hundred dollars that he lost. Backing away from the dice game he saw so much of his self in the kid.

As he walked backed over to his parked car he noticed his number two man awaiting him. Foe knew there was only one reason they ever meet and that was to make an exchange. After dapping hands with a closed fist, they embraced in a hood style hug. After making sure that no one wasn't paying the two of them any attention did Foe pop the trunk and pull out the last bag of cocaine that comprised half a kilo. Just as soon as he handed over the bag of cocaine did he take the win Dixie bag of money.

"How much is it?" Foe asked after shaking the bag up. The weight of it said that the money was good.

"That's $78,000.00. I'll have the other $22,000.00 before the night is out. Later on three small timers out of the Pork & Beans supposed to come grab some weight. So you can either slide back through later or pick the bread up in the morning when you come out."

Foe looked at his 4 series Apple watch to check the time. It was getting late and he has a hot date tonight with a special young lady.

"Nah I'll catch you in the morning. Just put everything up somewhere safe until the morning." He pauses for a second to read the incoming text on his watch. He had to admit that he was looking forward to his lovely date tonight. "Well, I'm out my boy. Hold everything down." Foe shouted out while making his way around the car to the driver side.

The two occupants, of the Jeep Grand Cherokee, stayed four car lengths away from their victim, as the passenger continued to text the person they were scoping out for the last two days. They both shared a laugh at how easy things are going for them.

The tint on the Jeep was so dark no one could see in even if they got close up on the windows. The two occupants had the inside of the truck flogged up with crack some. From the chain-smoking, they had been doing. Getting high and taking lives was something they loved to do. They know that they were supposed to stop smoking but the addiction was so real. They figured that the only way they'll get clean is if no more cocaine touches down in the city streets.

Behind the wheel of the Jeep was Snoop the calmer one of them two. Unlike Venom, he can focus on other things then killing when he's high. Like making sure that their vic goes exactly where they needed him to go without making any extra stops.

In the passenger, seat Venom was laying it on thick. Texting sexual things that would keep their victim excited. Whenever he would try and call the phone Venom would send him to voicemail and threaten to leave their meet-up spot if he try and call again. Like the sweet puppy he was, he stopped calling and followed along with whatever Venom said which their victim thought was the woman of his dreams.

"What a lame this guy is." Snoop joked while coughing from the thick grey smoke of crack cocaine that filled his lungs to capacity.

"Yea green as a pool table and twice as square. These young punks will do anything for some pussy." Venom said disgustedly from looking at what the man was texting who he thought was a stripper name Dolly Red.

They both set up straight in their seats when the yellow Challenger turned down US 27. Venom was glad that he took the bait because he didn't want to kill anyone else today. Just five more miles down the road and the Challenger should be pulling over to the side of the road where Dolly Red C 300 Benz is parked waiting on him.

After sitting the phone down Venom reached in the back seat and grabbed the bag of guns. Pulling out two Glock 40's then he twisted on the silencers. With the sun going down neither one of them were concerned about anyone seeing them put in work on their victim.

Just as they slowly approached the location Venom texted him telling him not to get out of the car. That she would make her way to him. Killing time as they parked a little ways down the street then started creeping up on him from behind. Swiftly and skillfully they moved through the bushes as if they were back in the army with the upper hand on the enemy.

Once they were 15 feet behind the Challenger did Venom text him again. This time telling him to exit the car and walk over to hers. To them it seemed like the moment he sent the text fool was bouncing out of his very own car. Before he could slam the door shut Snoop was all over him. One slap to the back of the head with the Glock and he was out cold. After quickly tying him up they tossed him inside the trunk of his own car. Venom took a cocktail bomb and threw it inside Dolly Red car. He left the driver door open so the fire could quickly spread. Before pulling off they made sure that no one had a chance to see their faces.

Once Venom and Snoop arrived at the abandoned house that they used to hog tie their victims they splashed a cup of hot water in Foe face. He woke up startle and his face was on fire. When Foe vision became clear standing before him was two of the cleanest fellas he'd every seen. Judging by their beat up grills and the crack rock stance that was wreaking off of their bodies he knew that they were crack heads. What he didn't know was what they wanted with him. He wasn't a corner hustle so there was no way the three of them could've ran in the same circle.

"Fuck you Jugs want?" Foe snapped while trying to break free, but the nylon rope didn't budge at all. No matter what he does there wasn't a thing he could do. His only shot at freedom is if they untie him.

Neither one of them said a word as Snoop held up a picture of Foe's boss.

"You fuck niggas got the wrong one. I ain't never been a snitch. I'll rather die before I give up my nigga. And he'll do the same for me. So eat a dick you fucking crack heads!" Foe shouted out at them. Raising his voice didn't move them at all as they both stood before him with a straight face.

Snoop nodded at Venom then he moved in on Foe. He grabbed a black bandanna off the plastic table then folded it up a few times before placing it over Foe eyes and tying it tight behind his head. After picking up a rubber ball Venom karate chopped him in the throat just to make him open his mouth wide enough to jam the ball in his mouth. There was no way Foe could spit the ball out or even cry out for help. By him not being able to close his wide-stretched mouth, the corners of his mouth will start to rip the dryer it gets. They figured that it shouldn't be any longer then 10 minutes until he's ready to tell God on Jesus. In their line of work they never seen anyone survive this.

They both took a seat and reloaded their crack pipes. After taking someone's life getting high was the second best thing that they both liked to do. They never been the ones to smoke anyone else crack, so they usually cook up their own crack. By the time they both took a blast Foe was already crying. They decided to let him feel it a little more because he tried to put on like he was gangsta.

Venom miss the old players of the game. The new school dealers and Killers are pedophiles and pussies. All they wanna do is act like the rappers. Back in their day the rappers wanted to be like the real hustlers.

They continued to get high as Foe cried out for help like the little bitch they knew he was without his gun. By now Foe had pissed and shitted his pants.

"Okay what you want to know about him?" Foe blurted out once Snoop had taking the ball out of his mouth. By now the corners of his mouth was raw from the lick of hydration.

"We want to know everything, and you better not hold back a thing." Venom threaten Him while holding up his famous surgical knife.

One look at the knife and Foe mouth just went to running. He didn't leave out a single detail. He spilled the beans on the whole drug organization on down to the names of his Boss Pitt Bulls.

Once Venom had heard enough he sliced Foe neck from ear to ear. Before wrapping up his lifeless body he made sure to cut his balls off. The City of Miami police would know that Foe was a pedophile When they find his body without his balls.

Before leaving the abandoned house they made sure they cleaned up any trace of Foe ever being there. They might be drug addicts, but they weren't stupid. Any links back to any of their victims will land them life in prison or the death penalty. Prison was out of the question for them there was no way they could smoke crack in a prison cell. So if it took them hours to clean up behind themselves then so be it they thought. Before locking up the place they both made plans to see Elihu in the morning.

CHAPTER ELEVEN

Don Royce has been sitting in front of his computer for the last three hours trying to see why his accounts don't add up with his inventory. The only thing he could think of was the guy Pete Wilson and his greed. As much money as he's kicking out to him he see no need to continue to run the number house and the couple of liquor stores he own in Miami.

With the money he has saved up and the money the restaurant is bringing in he can retire from the street life and live out the rest of his days stress free. Picking up the Boston Times paper the headline made his stomach flip upside down. On the cover stood his three old friends. They wouldn't call him their friend or brother. He figured that if he was being honest with himself they would love to see his head on a platter with his dick and balls in his own mouth.

Even though he's now living in Miami and going by a different name. With the types of resources they have he figured that it won't be long before they find him and put a hit out on his and his wife head. From this day forward his security detail will be beefed up.

Sitting the paper down and leaning back in his plush leather chair with his hands over his eyes. He knew this day would come but it seem like it came around to fast. All he could do now is man up.

Carla hates to see her husband have a nervous breakdown. The man that she married wasn't afraid of a soul. She has no idea who he is now, so she walked over to him and did what any real wife would've done. She slapped him clean across the face. "I know damn well you ain't afraid of them. You made your decision to make the moves you made. Now you have to live with that. Now get off your ass and show all these pussies you're still not to be fucked with. First you need to start off with this black bastard that keep coming around here collecting our money as if he worked for it." She waited to see his reaction. She knew that he didn't know that she knew what was going on. "Yea I been knew. Now the next time he try to come in here you need to put a bullet in that bastard head. Be the fucking man that I married." She yelled out then zoomed out of his office. Knowing that she planted a seed inside of him that will make him come out of retirement.

It was like something washed over him after his wife slapped him and said just the right words to him. So he picked up his cellphone and dialed a number that he would've never thought he'll have use for.

"Hello this is Don Royce and I was wondering if you can stop by the restaurant today by any chance?"

"Yea I can stop by is 4:45 pm good for you?" The person on the other end of the phone replied to him.

"Yea see you then." Don Royce replies then he hung the phone up. Looking at the ancient clock on the wall above his book shelf He had one hour and a half before he shows up. He figured he could kill some time with his wife until then.

Today was the day of the week that Agent Coleman has to report with her boss and turn over everything that she learned so far about the Dominguez Cartel. With a cup of strong coffee from Starbucks in her hand, she entered the conference room with her two fellow field agents. The other two were really enjoying this operation being that they were not trying to bust anyone.

Special agent Aaron Kirkland was full of energy. Instead of having a seat like everyone else he just paced back and forward in front of the bulletin board.

"So ladies any word on the Cartel as of yet?"

"No, not a single word. Hasn't even mention the fact that he also knows who Gustavo Dominguez is. I really feel like we are beating a dead horse, sir. From what I see Elihu is just spending a lot of time with family and friends." Agent Coleman feels like the FBI is wasting taxpayers money on a case that's going nowhere.

"We just have to dig deeper. Maybe we should plant bugs in his home and tap his phones. Yea we're going to bug his home. I need you to plant bugs all around his house. He has something up his sleeve and I'm determined to find out what it is. Before you leave Agent Coleman collect those bugs from the front desk. And ladies keep up the good work. I promise to see to it myself that all three of you get the promotions that you so much deserve." With that said he rushed all three of them out of his office.

As she exited the conference room she couldn't help but feel like things will get flipped on Elihu. Being an FBI agent herself she was very familiar with these tactics that the FBI like to use against black men. Doing her job never bothered her when the person of interest was a suspect. In Elihu case, he was targeted because of who his roommate was in prison. She somehow keep telling herself that Elihu may not have a clue who the leader of the Cartel is. Like why would the Mexicans tell him? He's not Mexican and they only deal with their own kind she thought to herself.

With so much attitude she grabbed the bag of high tic bugs then made her way out of the building.

After the last time, Elihu saw Don Royce he would've never thought he would ever hear from him again. He figured that he'll show up being that he asked him to show up. On the way over to the restaurant, he soaked in everything that Snoop and Venom had for him. Thanks to them it won't be long before they get this nigga Pete Wilson out the way. As gruesome as these two are he's glad to have them on his side of the playing field.

Once David pulled up to the front of the restaurant did Elihu end the phone call with his two unchained Gorillas. Before leaving the Bentley truck he explained to David to keep the engine running. He didn't expect to be long in the restaurant. To be honest with himself he doesn't know what made him agree to come and sit down with the Don. He figured that it must have been the fact that Don Royce reached out to him.

Dressed in a all white linen suit with his dreads wrapped up in a white turbine. His Cologne fragrance for today was by Creed. On his feet was the most comfortable pair of loafers he brought from an African shop. The loafers were so light on his feet he found himself looking down at his feet a few times just to make sure he didn't walk out of the house wearing his bedroom shoes.

Just like any other time he steps into a place with a crowd of people his presents alone demand the full attention of everyone around. He was the definition of what a real man should move like or even carry himself.

As he made his way to Don Royce office he nodded and smiled at the onlookers showing off his pearly white teeth. Once in the kitchen area, he felt like the spotlight wasn't on him anymore.

The hostess Knocked on the office door and let the Don know that Elihu was here to see him. Elihu could hear the Don yell from the inside to allow him into the office. Once the hostess opened up the door did Elihu make his way inside.

"Thanks for showing up on so short notice. Please have a seat tho Elihu." He motioned for what chair he wanted him to sit in.

"What do I owe for this social call? Our last encounter wasn't so great. Did you call me down here to beat me down about the mistake I asked you forgiveness for?" He figured that he should at least throw that out there. Because that was the only thing Don Royce could hold over his head.

Instead of responding to Elihu he picked up the newspaper while showing him the article writing about the last Don's of Boston. "Do you know who those guys are Elihu?"

"Yes, trouble for you. I read on you guys while I was locked away. I needed to know what I was up against. I know that you changed your name and that your Mob brothers feel that you turned your back on them. They even think you turned them over to authorities For your freedom. Should I keep going?"

Don Royce held his hand up. "No say no more. I hate to even relive the past in my head." He grabbed a manila folder from next to his computer. Opened it up and pulled out a single picture. Placing it in front of Elihu he was shocked not to get any reaction from him.

"What about him?" Elihu finally asked. He was also familiar with the fact that Pete Wilson was taxing everyone who wasn't straight and narrow.

"He's a pain in my back." Don Royce held his hand up stopping Elihu from cutting him off. "I can care less about the street life. All I want to do is run my restaurant. The game has never been good to me. So I'm asking that you take over as the Don. There has never been a black Don before." Don Royce pulled his commission ring off of his finger. Not once since he made Don have he ever taken the ring off. "Maybe this ring can do more for you then it's ever done for me. My time is minimal. With this ring in your possession you can claim that you stripped me because of the things I have done." He pushed the ring closer to Elihu. He didn't make an attempt to pick it up. "You have to protect this ring. No city streets is safe if they have all four rings. As long as you have the ring you will have a voice. You don't think I know that you need Pete dead so you can take over the drug trade down her in Florida. With this ring, you'll be able to accomplish that and more. This is your chance to be a Boss of all Bosses."

Elihu finally picked the ring up. His fingers were to big for the ring. "A man in your position was too weak to have so much power but I'll gladly take the ring off of your fingers-" the sound of his ringing cellphone caught him off guard. Elihu took that opportunity to exit Don Royce office.

"Elihu I need for you to make sure that my restaurant is protected. Me and my wife don't mind living in hiding. Keep all harm away from here."

"I'll make sure that everyone knows to stay away from here." He lied while making his exit. Looking at his caller ID the name on the screen made him stop in his tracks and accept the call. "Hello is everything okay?"

"No everything is not ok. How fast can you get to the truck stop? I need to speak with you face to face."

Looking at his watch it was still early. He had maybe two more hours before rush hour traffic. "I'll be there in 30 min." He said into the phone before rushing outside to his waiting truck. "Take me to my kid's mom truck stop asap." He explained to David while shutting the door behind himself.

CHAPTER TWELVE

The message that was delivered with Foe's body was clear and uncut. There was a new player on the board. Pete couldn't believe his eyes as he looked down at his wife nephew. His eyes had been removed and replace with his testicles. Not once in his 45 years of life has he ever saw something so gruesome.

Pete put on a pair of gloves then removed the envelope that was stuck to Foe bloody chest. After opening it he begins to read the lines.

"Your times as the head honcho is running out. Do the world a favor and put a bullet in your own head."

Pete blood pressure quickly shot through the roof. He's never been disrespected in such a way. For the last ten years that he's been in the drug trade, he never lost a single Soldier.

"Within the next 48 hours, I want the heads of whoever was responsible for this. If I don't have any answers soon I will think hard about replacing you all. These city streets belong to us. If one of you don't feel that way please step forward so I can put a fucking bullet in your fucking head right now." Pete was holding onto the butt of his 357 Magnum so tight everyone thought he would crush the wood handle. "Now get the fuck outta my face and don't come back until you killed whoever crossed the line."

Once everyone was gone did he cover up Foe's body. Placing his gun back in she shoulder holster then he pulled out his Apple iPhone. He dreaded this phone call, but it has to be made. The sweet sound of his wife's voice sent chills up his spine. Usually, her voice sounded just like a melody of a beautiful love song.

"Bae you might wanna sit down for this one. Someone killed Foe. They cut his balls off and plucked his eye's out. They went as far as placing his testicles in his eye sockets. It's horrible bae. They didn't have to do him like that. Killing him was one thing but they didn't have to degrade him." He dropped his head. Her silence was doing something to him. He promised that he would protect their whole family and that no harm would come close to the family at all.

"Just have someone drop the body off to the morgue. I shouldn't have to tell you what to do. Because right now how I'm feeling it's fuck that Mayor shit. That hit had to come from that bitch Saudy. She must be upset with you because you limiting her drug supply into the Miami ports. I want that bitch head. She's responsible for my nephew death. Ain't nobody else around stupid enough to touch anyone in this family." She snapped through the phone then hung it up in his face.

Taking a seat he had a lot to think about. His last conversation with Saudy didn't go so well. He had taking a trip out to Mexico with the head of the last person she tried to do business with. He had made it clear to her that whoever from the states wanted to do business with the Cartel had to order through him. He planned to be the sole link to Mexico. He could tell that she was pissed but she had no other choice or risk trying to get her cocaine in through another port. All the southern port already belonged to different crime families.

It's been over two years since he had to take a head to Mexico, so he canceled her from the equation. Deep down inside he felt in his heart that whoever was responsible for Foe's untimely death was from right here in Miami. He thought back to when his men first brought Foe body in the house he asked them did he have his cellphone on him. Come to find out he didn't. He remembers his last conversation with Foe he would meet with a young lady friend.

Pete quickly calls T-Mobile and have them email him a print out of his call log and his most recent text message. Not even a minute later

T-Mobile was sending the documents. While going through the call log he noticed that Foe made a call, but the person never picked up. He found a long conversation over text with that same person Dolly Red. Just reading the text he knew that it was a setup. The person doesn't answer the phone because it wasn't Dolly Red who he was talking to. Pete couldn't believe how stupid Foe was.

Jotting down the number as he text the meet-up address of Foe and Dolly Red to his soldiers. All he needed was a small clue to lead him in the right direction.

After waiting for over 30 minutes he finally received a call back from one of his soldiers. They found a car burned to crisp. The police were investigating the murder of Dolly Red. Her body was found in the trunk of her car poorly burned. He explained to Pete that Foe was the main suspect. Her cellphone was found with her purse and drivers license about 20 feet from her roasted vehicle.

Pete slammed his cellphone to the ground. He knew for sure now that someone set Foe up. He would get to the bottom of this even if it kills him.

✈✈✈✈✈

Before David could bring the truck to a complete stop Elihu was jumping out the back seat. Not knowing what to expect but he still rushed inside Lisa's office. "Lisa!" He screamed out from fear of the worst happening to her or their kids.

"I'm out back." She replied to him.

He rushed through the double doors that led to the parked Rigs and a small gas station that she also owns. He could tell that she was doing ok by all the shops that sat on her property.

"Where you at though?" He yelled out somewhat tired of looking for her. There were too many parked trucks and there was no way he was about to check them all.

Lisa stepped out from between a yellow and a green Rig. "Right here. Come see this." Once she was sure that he saw her did she shoot back in between the trucks.

Elihu jogged over to her. "So what are we looking for?" Looking up at her as she stood in the middle of the open trailer doors all he could do was admire her beauty. With age, her body seemed to develop really nicely. Her track star legs where thick and her ass was still round like a bubble. She looked magnificent.

"Can you climb up here? Or are you too old?" She joked. She hated to admit that she was still attracted to him. He was the only man that she has known since middle school. She gave him her innocence and he cheated with a white chick. Just as quickly as the heat flashes came over her they were gone just like that and she couldn't stand the sight of him again.

With one leap Elihu was in the trailer. "What seems to be the problem? I don't see any threat here."

"I called you because this is the third trailer that I found with a stash spot in it. Someone is trafficking drugs in my trucks." She couldn't believe the very words that came out of her mouth. For years she has run a clean business. She never even had a run-in with the cops.

"Ok, but what does this have to do with me? I ain't put it there." He was just as lost as she was.

She hated to feel the way she was feeling right now. "I think Eric is trafficking drugs. I have caught him in the truck stop late at night before. I just can't prove it."

Elihu refused to believe that a 14-year-old is trafficking drugs unless he's doing it for someone else. "Slow down you have to make some sense of what you saying to me. Our son is 14 years old. Who does he hang out with that could possibly want to transport this much of anything. You tripping blaming it on our son."

"Elihu you don't know your son like that. He was running with the Bloods when he was only ten years old. Maybe they put him up to it. He's sneaky just like you. Your fucking twin." She yelled out as she broke down crying and beating on Elihu.

He let her get it out while thinking about the impression he got from both his kids. Neither one of them struck him as bad or troubled kids. He will have a serious sit-down with their son real soon. There was no way he would let his son get wrapped up in any gang.

"Lisa you have to really think about what you are saying. That son of ours ain't stupid enough to let someone ship anything in your Rigs. What I wanna know is who you had to get rid of the last trailer you found with the hidden compartment." Elihu could tell that she wasn't in her right frame of mind and that could cause her not to think straight. At this very moment though he needed her to weigh all of her options.

"I had my husband get rid of the trailer. I had him hire a security company to make sure that no one tries to add cargo on the trailers. All it takes is for one state trooper to pull over one of my trucks and find that hidden compartment for them to have the local authority raid my truck stop." She didn't know what to do. What she did know was that Elihu was the perfect person to help her get to the bottom of this problem she has. "You gotta help me."

Stepping back for a moment while he ran his right hand down his long and thick beard. "So the last time you found one of these trailers you had your husband get rid of it. Did he ever tell you where he took the trailer?"

She just stood there shaking her head trying to weave through her memories. "Yea he said something about taking it to another truck stop and selling it for our money back." She replied to him with a puzzled look on her face. "What does that have to do with anything."

"Wheres he at now?"

"Some kind of business meeting. Maybe six months ago he decided to start his own business. Once a week he comes here and checks up on trucks with his personal mechanic." As the words were flowing out of her mouth she realized something. "He's coming this afternoon. Like clockwork, he will show up around 2:30 or 3:00 pm. The last two times I found a truck was either on a Monday night or Tuesday morning. I'll kill him if he's jeopardizing my business. I worked too hard to build up a good rep with the local truck drivers and the Police."

"Let's not jump to conclusions just yet. Maybe it's not him and someone is trying to frame him for it. So instead of telling anyone what you found today. Just watched this truck closely. Whoever is either loading this truck or picking it up to be loaded will show their face. You'll know who's responsible soon enough." The last thing he wanted her to think was that he was hating on her husband. So he climbed down from the trailer. Then helped her down.

"I'm going to watch this truck and trailer like a hawk. Ain't nothing getting passed me today. Just wait and see." She told him as she locked the trailer door back shut.

An awkward silence fell over the two of them as they walked back in the direction of the front office. Elihu had to admit that he was proud of the businesswoman she became over the years. The old Lisa that he remembered just wanted to follow him and get into whatever he wanted to do.

"I have to admit you doing pretty good for yourself." He admitted finally.

She playfully giggled. "Well, actually it was the money you left that made this all possible. Five million dollars can only go so fast. I figured that I'll open a business that would provide for me and the twins. Jeff came along and help me out a lot. He's the reason the truck stop is doing so well. He's very business minded. You two should really sit down and get to know each other. He's also great with the twins. I must say I thank God for him."

Elihu was just about to comment on how she feels about this Jeff guy when the sound of his ringing phone broke his train of thoughts. Charlene's name and picture displayed on the screen. "Excuse me I have to take this call." He explained while taking three or four steps away from Lisa for privacy. "Good afternoon beautiful. I'm kinda tied up right now speaking with Lisa the twin's mom."

"Oh, it's okay. I was only calling because I want you to come over to my place tonight. I wanna cook up a special meal for you. Unless you have other plans tonight?"

"No I'm free. Is 7:30 or 8:00 good for you?" He asked not once looking back at the impression on Lisa's face. Straight jealousy was in her eyes. By the time he wrapped the phone call up Lisa was standing there like she didn't have a problem with him dating so soon.

Unable to hold it she blurted out at him, "You just can't give yourself time to enjoy your freedom. You just have to be in a relationship.

You need to focus more on building a relationship with the twins instead of some female." She just shook her head in disgust. "You something else."

He didn't see what the big problem was with him having a lady friend. He felt as though he was entitled to a life his self. "You tripping. I spend nothing but time with the twins. Since I been home I been in their life." He had to catch himself there was no way he would argue with her. He decided to brush her off and leave. He figured that would be the best thing that he could do. He was no fool Lisa was jealous of him moving on. He left her standing there looking dumbfounded.

CHAPTER THIRTEEN

As Don Royce made his rounds around his lavish restaurant he forced himself to appear like his old self. Knowing that his days were numbered really was eating at him. His health seemed to be worse than it's ever been before. For some odd reason, he has been feeling pain in his joints. He didn't know if it was just a mind thing or if he was really hurting. He made a mental note to take a trip to the doctor's office soon.

Just as he checked on the last table of diners he noticed His wife Carla standing in the kitchen doorway. The look on her face wasn't pleasant. She nodded for him to look toward the front door when he did look standing there were five Italians dressed and grey suits. When he looked back at his wife she had tears in her eyes.

There was no need for him to run. If the front door was covered then each exit of the restaurant was covered with goons. He slowly walked towards her. Once in the kitchen, everything was still taking place as if nothing was about to take place. No one had a clue that Don Royce and Carla's life is very much in danger.

Before stepping into his office he wiped the tears from his wife's eyes. He refused to let anyone see either of them cry. Holding hand and hand they made their way into the office. To his surprise, neither of his old friends were in attendance. Sitting behind his desk was the youngest son of Don George family. Standing in the opposite corner of the office was Don Donald only son. Don Freddy daughter was the only female in the room other than Carla.

"Robert McCoy, you know why we're here right?" asked Don Freddy daughter Jane.

Don Royce had heard a lot about her and none of what he heard was good. She is a fierce Killer. Word is you'll rather jump in front of a bullet train than have a negative run-in with her.

"Our fathers feel that your time here on earth has to end tonight. So you have two choices. You can either drink this liquid or allow us to place two bullets into the back of each of your heads. Before we get into that part we would love for you to turn over your ring for the commission." Don Donald youngest son Nicolas asked while looking at Don Royce hands and neck. The ring was nowhere in sight.

"Where the fuck is the ring?" Don George son Murphy asked also noticing that he doesn't have the ring.

"You can kill us, but your families will never have complete control of the east coast." Don Royce said while looking, Murphy in the eyes then he quickly picked up the drank. His reaction was so fast neither of them couldn't get to him fast enough. By the time they did he had drunk the whole bottle of poison. The toxin didn't take long to kick in. His body jerked back and forward a few times as he choked trying his best to breath. Not even a minute later he was bleeding from his nose and eye sockets.

"Fuck poison her also. Fuck.... Fuck.... Fuck." Murphy didn't want to fly back home without that ring. There was nothing left for him to do. Taking a seat in Don Royce chair as the goons held Carla down and force the poison down her throat.

They watched as she fraught a little harder than Don Royce did. But it wasn't long before the poison consumed her Immune system and she was choking and gasping for air. After ordering one of the goons to check them both for a pulse and found none. They quickly wrapped them up and carried their bodies out the back door.

✗✗✗✗✗

After cleaning himself up Elihu drove himself to Charlene condo. He had to admit he was impressed with her taste. Her place was laced with the finer things. He figured either her last dude was in the drug game or she was. Must of the designer furniture belonged in a mansion on south beach. His antennas went through the roof when he laid eyes on the marble bathroom.

His conversation with Lisa kind of helped open his eyes. He was definitely sweet on Charlene, but now he has a million questions for her. He could only hope that she has been keeping it real with him.

He stopped and admired the collage of pictures that rested over the fake fireplace. He couldn't help but notice that there wasn't a single picture of her childhood years up there. From what he could tell all the picture couldn't be any over one month old. She was wearing the same hairstyle in each picture. The same exact hairstyle she was wearing when they first met. He found that very odd.

"I hope you're starving because I think I cooked too much food." She jokingly asked as she put the final touches on the meal that she was whipping up for him.

"Yea I'm definitely starving. It smells excellent in here also." If He didn't care about anything else in this world. His family and food were the top things on his list.

"Well, the food is ready. What would you like to drink? I have bottled water, fruit punch, and champagne." She asked as she sat the last dish of food on the round table for four.

"Water would be great. This is a nice place that you have here. You must make a pretty penny at work to afford these things."

She froze for a moment when she grabbed the bottle of water. She only hoped that he didn't recognize this place because it was seized by the FBI. She really didn't think things through before she invited him over. She brushed things off as if she must be tripping. She figured that there was no way Elihu could possibly know who this place belonged to. The site had been seized while he was still serving time in prison.

"I did tell you I have my own Realtors business right. My clientele is very exclusive. On average, I flip at least five homes in a month. Would you like to say a prayer for the food?" She asked trying to change the subject making sure to keep her tone even.

"Yea I'll say a prayer." With a smile on his face, he reached both of his hands out and grabbed hers. "Let's bow our heads. Father God I'll like to thank you for this beautiful meal that you allowed Charlene to prepare for us tonight. I pray that I'll enjoy her cooking especially if I will be keeping her around for a while. Amen!"

"Amen." She repeated after him. She could tell that something was bothering him. He seemed a little distanced for some strange reason. She figured that she'll have him eating out the palm of her hand. She was wearing her natural hair in a wrap. The soft gold fitted dress that she was wearing huge her every curve. Underneath she didn't have on a stench of panties or even a bra.

"Is everything ok?" she finally asked after eating in silence for at least 5 minutes.

"Yea I'm good. I'm enjoying the meal. I really appreciate the fact that you cooked for me." He replied then sat his fork down. He was receiving a text from Venom. After reading it he excused himself to the restroom. Leaving his phone behind sitting next to his plate on the table.

As soon as she heard the bathroom door close and lock she was all in his phone reading texts and searching for any clues who is controlling the Dominguez Cartel. One part of her hoped and wish that she didn't find a thing, then, on the other hand, she needed to know. After collecting a couple of suspicious things from his phone. She set it back down where he left it and played it off like she never moved an inch. After hearing the toilet flush and the sink water running she knew it wouldn't be long before he walked out of the bathroom.

Making his way back to the table while drying his hands with a paper towel. He took one look at his phone and knew that she had been through it. What she didn't realize is that the screen doesn't go to sleep for five minutes. Looking at the time on his iced out Rolex, he figured that he should've had at least two more minutes before his screen would've gone to sleep. He made a mental note not to say anything to her about it right now. He didn't wonder what division she was working for. Was it DEA, CIA, or the FBI. Whoever she worked for he wonders why they were sticking close to him. He served his time and he didn't go to prison for selling any drugs or Gang activities.

He figured that for now, he'll ease the tension in the room by creating small talk. Within minutes he had her laughing at his jokes. He needed her to remain comfortable while he finds out what's really going on.

After diner, she got just what she was looking for. Elihu putting a hurting on her like he does best. They went at it all night. Each time driving her crazier then the round before. He had her drunk off of his lovemaking. By the time they both fell asleep she had too much on her brain and not that much time to really think things through. She figured that she'll just take things one step at a time. After taking one last look at his handsome face she knew right then and there that Elihu was the man for her. With a warm smile on her face, she snuggled up under his arms and fell straight to sleep.

Lisa was determined to find out who really is responsible for the hidden compartments in her trailers. Looking at her wristwatch and it was after 9 pm. The overnight security team had clocked in and not even a minute later her husband Jeff Range Rover pulled into the truck stop followed by a minivan. She couldn't believe her eyes. The man that she grew to love was using her truck to traffic drugs and only God knows what else.

Taking out her phone she zoomed in and snapped a couple of pictures of the crew loading the trailer with cocaine. She recognized the gentleman standing next to Jeff. As many times as she saw his face on the television screen, but not once has she seen him around the Truck Stop. She figured that he had to be muscling Jeff into trafficking the drugs for him.

She quickly shot the pictures to Elihu phone. Calling the cops was out of the question because she figured the soon to be Mayor had a few on his payroll. Just as she pocketed her phone and tried to stand up and leave she was noticed by two security guards.

"Freeze don't fucking move!" One of the guards yelled out gathering everyone else attention.

In a flash, she was surrounded by security guards. Jeff and soon to be Mayor Pete came walking around the Rig. With tears in her eyes, she looked up at the man that she had been giving her heart to for years. The look in his eyes said that he could only fear what will happen to her next.

"How could you Jeff? So this is the other business that you started. You a drug dealer now huh?" She snapped. She wanted to kill him with her bare hands.

"You should've gone home. Now you force my hand. Baby, I was trying to keep you in the blind. You just had to be nosey." He just shook his head and walked away. He knew that Pete would never let her live knowing that she can connect him to drugs. So he did what he thought would be the best thing for him to do and that was walking away. Tears were running down his face as the staged security guards gave her a good beat down. A single gunshot followed shortly. He really loved her, but this was business. If he would've fought for her there would be two dead bodies laid out right now instead of one.

Jeff climbed behind the wheel of his Range Rover then pulled away. He had some explaining to do to the kids. He planned to see what Pete does with her body first before he says a thing to anyone. After wiping away his tears he stepped down on the gas real hard. He drove through the city streets like a bat out of hell with no regard for human life. His heart was cold now. Just a moment ago the only woman that ever showed him, true love, was murdered and there wasn't a thing that he could've done about it.

CHAPTER FOURTEEN

The next morning when Elihu awakened he was butt ass naked in Charlene's bed. The smell of Turkey bacon grits and eggs was in the air. He sat up straight then checked his phone for the time only to find that Lisa had texted him last night. After taking his hand and cleaning out the sleep from around his eyes he opened the phone and checked his messages. After taking a good look at the pictures he decided to call her phone. He knew that she had to be hurting inside right now. Her own husband was the one responsible for trafficking drugs through her Rigs.

After calling her over four times and she never picked up. He decided to call Venom and Snoop. While the phone ringed in his ear he walked over to the door to make sure that Charlene was still in the kitchen. Seeing that the coast was clear he backed away from the door.

"What's good big homie?" Venom asked wondering why Elihu would be calling them this early in the morning.

"Are y'all still following this nigga Pete?"

"Yea around the clock. Last night they made a stop by Lisa's Truck stop. Why is everything straight?"

"Fuck no everything ain't straight. She sent me a couple of pictures of them loading her Rigs with cocaine. Now she ain't picking up her phone. Send Snoop to check and see if her car is still parked out there." Elihu was trying not to raise his voice because he didn't need Charlene to sneak up and hear his conversation.

"I will get him on it now." Venom has been knowing Elihu for far too long he instantly knew when something was wrong with him. He noticed that Elihu was trying to remain calm but the uneven tone in his voice said so much to Venom. He knew that his friend was hurting badly about this one. Venom knew that if something serious happened to Lisa there would be no turning back for Elihu. He would make sure that the streets feel the same pain that he would have to endure.

"Thanks, bruh. I'll catch y'all later though." Elihu hung the phone up then set it down on the nightstand.

Charlene had walked up halfway through Elihu conversation. She also knew him well enough to know that there was a severe problem. She had heard enough to know that something big was taking place. She might have nothing on the cartel, but she does have enough to have a field agent follow carefully behind him.

She slowly walked back to the kitchen with the tray of food. "Baby, you up?" She yell out acting like she could hear him moving around in the room.

"Yea. The food smells really good." He replied while heading into the kitchen nude. He knew this would get a reaction out of her.

"So daddy brought breakfast for mama also." She jokingly said while playing with his balls in her hand, while kissing him passionately.

With no effort he scooped her off of her feet and sat her down on top of the kitchen countertop. Sitting there she fed him his breakfast. Once he was good and full did he allow her to have her breakfast afterward. Once they finished their morning round of lovemaking they to a shower then went their separate ways with different agendas then what they told each other.

✗✗✗✗✗

Charlene better known as agent Rashonda Coleman walked inside the Federal Government building with mixed emotions. She was a agent at heart but for some strange reason she felt like she was wrong for carrying out what she planned to do. Elihu wasn't a suspect but here she was ready to build a case on him without any concrete evidence against him.

She wanted to turn around and just walk back out the door, but she had already sent in pictures of everything that she found in his phone. She had some explaining to do and she doesn't know where to start.

Once she stepped foot in her department all eyes seemed to be on her for some strange reason. She paid the stares no mind because no one knew her situation. Looking ahead inside the glass conference room sitting before the three special agents sat agent Shipmen. From the looks of things, they looked to be drilling her.

From where she stood she tried to play nonchalant as if she didn't know what was going on with Agent Shipmen. Five minutes later they had kicked agent Shipment out of the office. She shot right pass Rashonda as if she wasn't standing there.

"Agent Coleman you can come in now." Yelled out the leading Special Agent that sat in between the other two.

"Good morning." She said using her welcoming voice. She was the one with the news but for some strange reason she felt like she was on trial.

"Agent Coleman do you know the reason for me calling you in here today?" Asked the head man.

"Is it because of the pictures I sent to the head of my department?" She asked while looking to her boss for help. All she found was a blank expression on his face.

"Yea and no. You know that I have to suspend you, and everyone involved with this bogus case that y'all have created against Elihu. If he finds out that his home is bugged along with his cellphone he'll be able to sue the pants off of this department. You have 24 hours to get the bugs outta his home. We have already removed the tap off of his phone. Once you turn in the bugs your suspension starts Immediately. Three weeks from now and you'll be able to come back to work. Do you understand what I've said to you agent Coleman?"

"Yes, sir I understand you clearly." She confirmed but never removing her eyes from her leading agent.

"You are excused."

She stood up from her seat then left out of the conference room. Shortly after she was walking out of the building. Before climbing behind the wheel of her car she spotted this red Chevy Malibu parked up the street. The car looked very familiar. She could've sworn that she noticed the car from when she left her home this morning. After climbing behind the wheel of her car did the Chevy make a U-turn and head the opposite way. Her Intuition told her that the car had to been following her. Brushing it off for now as she pulled away from the building.

Before leaving Charlene house Elihu texted Kimberly and asked that she bring his kids to the big house. He needed to find out everything he could on this Jeff guy. Not too long ago Snoop had texted him explaining that Lisa's car was still parked in her regular spot and the engine was very cold as if she hasn't started the car in hours. At that very moment, he feared for the worst for his twin's mom.

Things are about to go left so Elihu gave David a couple of weeks off with pay. He allowed David to take any car of his choice with $50,000.00. He didn't want the kid around right now. Things might get dangerous for him. The last thing he wanted was to be the cause of the kid death.

Once he whipped the Bentley truck in front of his parents home he damn near breaks the transmission by cutting the truck off so fast. In a flash, he was inside his parents home.

"Is everything okay son?" Asked Anthony Sr. He knew that look on his son's face all too well. Something had to be terribly wrong.

"Lisa's dead. She's not picking up her phone and her car is still parked at the truck stop."

Erica heard every word that her father said. "What!!!" She broke down to her knees. She refused to believe that her best friend in the entire world was dead and gone.

Elihu had no idea that she was standing there. This was not how he wanted to explain this to his kids. He rushed to her side as everyone else entered the kitchen trying to figure out why Erica was crying uncontrollably. "I'm so sorry baby." He whispered in her ear while he consoled her. The cat was completely out of the bag now. One look at Eric and he understood. Elihu watched as his son took off running. After motioning for Kimberly to get Erica did Elihu take off behind his son. He found him out back standing by the pool.

"It was that dude Jeff, huh?" Eric asked as he turned around to face his father. "You know mom thought I was responsible for trafficking in her Rigs. I'll never do her like that. But one time I did catch that dude doing some funny shit one night. I never said a thing to mom because he was walking around with that dude Pete Wilson. A couple of my gang brothers say that Pete is the one supplying the whole city. I should've said something to her then. It's all my fault that she ain't here anymore. I should've said something dad."

"It's not your fault son. What was meant to happen will happen? But what I need from you right now is the wear about of Jeff. I need you to call him and ask about your mom. Try to get him to meet with you. Can you do that for me?"

"Yes, sir." Eric pulled out his phone and called Jeff. He made sure to set up a time for them to meet.

Elihu called Snoop and gave him the time and place where Jeff is scheduled to meet Eric. They made plans to grab him then. After the call, Elihu and Eric made their way back in the house to greave with the rest of the family.

CHAPTER FIFTEEN

Elihu had an amazing conversation with his son Eric and he was proud of the young man that he was becoming. Realizing that his son was far too gone when it came down to the street life he figured the best thing to do is bring him even closer to him. There was no way he would allow anyone to influence Eric on how to be street. Eric is his son and he vowed to teach him how to be a boss.

For now, he was headed over to his home to meet with Charlene. He had already received confirmation about her being Fed. When he first got the news he wanted to have Venom and Snoop get rid of her, but the love he has for her is so real. He figured once everything blows over with Jeff and Pete, he'll question her about her affiliation with the FBI.

When he pulled up to his estate he found her parked outside his security gate waiting on him. Pressing the buzzer allowing them both to enter the property. Once out front of the house, he parked directly behind her. Climbing out of his truck he took in every inch of her. She was flawless. In his 30 plus years on earth, he never came across a woman that could stand next to her. He definitely knew right then that letting her go was out of the question.

"Elihu I have some explaining to do." She cried out only for him to silence her.

"No need to speak on it. I already know. My question to you is. Who side are you going to stand on when everything hit the fan. Are you going to be my woman Rashonda or agent, Charlene? The choice is yours. I'm not a suspect in the Federal Government eyes. So are you going to build a case on me or rock with me?" He needed to know where they stood. No matter what choice she decides to make really doesn't matter to him. If she makes the wrong choice the next time he sees her he'll have no choice but to kill her. Just thinking about killing the woman that he loves made him feel sick to the stomach.

"I chose you. I love you Elihu Israel. The Feds are not building any case on you. Never have and they're still not. But please forgive me for misleading you. But I need to get a couple things out of your home."

"Those bugs are in the garage packed away in plastic shopping bag. I had David search the house for them last night. The move you made at the dinner table said it all. But we passed all that. Now we can build for the future. I'm gonna set you up real nice. Them crackers can't give you nothing compared to what I can do for you." He explained to her while whipping the tears from her eyes.

"I'm with you baby."

"We're going to take a trip later. So go grab your things and get ready for tonight. I'll call you when I'm ready. I got a few things to handle first."

She knew just what he was talking about. She overheard his conversation earlier with his friend over the phone. "Baby do you have to go. Can you let someone else handle those things for you? Whatever it is you have to do that is."

Elihu gave her his signature look as if he knew she knew more then what she was hinting at. He figured if she did know she had to have been eavesdropping when she was supposed to be preparing breakfast. "Rashonda just do as I said. The less you know the better." He told her then climbed back behind the wheel of his truck.

Pete just received the phone call that his shipment of cocaine didn't make it to Jacksonville, Florida. He promised that the shipment will arrive before the night is out. He figured that the driver must have had a problem on the road. Quickly searching through his phone for Jeff's number. He appointed Jeff in charge of the drivers, so he better have answers for him, or he will end up fish food just like his wife.

After calling him over two times and he never picked up he wanted blood. "Round up the troops. We going hunting." Pete refused to let anyone run off with his drugs or his money.

The sound of his ringing cellphone startled him. He answered the phone without looking at the screen thinking Jeff was calling back. "You better have some answers for me."

"I figured that you would have some for me, Mr. Mayor." The sweet voice on the other end of the phone said to him.

His blood was boiling now. Saudy never makes phone calls. So he found it kind of odd she'll call him on a day like this. The same day his shipment comes up missing. "You know that you'll never get another gram of cocaine in this port again."

"And no one will ever sell you a gram again. So how much money you have to pay back to your buyer in Jacksonville? More money than you probably can afford to pay back. Without me, you will be broke in no time. You played with me like a dog long enough. I just had to call you and tell you myself. You no more have total control of anything." With that said she hung the phone up in his face.

Without cocaine, his control of the streets will be over soon. Picking up the bottle of Remy then he turned it upside down. He was ruined and he didn't have any idea who was taking his place. He vowed to find out and make them pay.

It's been over 12 hours since Lisa had been murdered and Jeff hasn't slept at all. Every time he tried to close his eyes and get some rest his last image of Lisa would pop up. He figured that she was haunting him for allowing Pete and his goons to kill her.

He felt like a chump because he should've protected him. It was her that showed him love when no else did. Letting them kill her was him taking the butch way out he thought. He saw Pete calling him. He was in the mood to talk with him just yet. When Eric called he had no choice but to answer. If he didn't he figured that he'll make himself look guilty. Eric explained that he wanted to meet. He had been having problems with the bloods again was what he told him. Jeff couldn't see how a good kid like Eric would even get mixed up with an organized gang anyway. Never the less he planned to help the kid out as best as he could. Besides his mother ain't here to help him out anymore.

When his cellphone vibrated Eric had texted him letting him know that he was pulling up to the address. Jeff rushed to the window just to see who all was coming with the kid. The only car out front was the Uber that Eric had climbed out of. Unsure of what was really going on Jeff left the door locked until Eric was standing on the doorstep. In a flash, he unlocked the door and swung it open allowing his stepson to enter the house. Quickly locking the door behind Eric then he turned around to face him on to come face to face with the blackish and roughest looking man that was pointing a gun straight at him.

"Hey what the fuck is going on here?" Jeff asked while raising his hands over his head. He didn't want to die like this but the look he saw in the man eyes read nothing but death.

"What have you done with my mother? And don't lie we got pictures of you and the Soon to be Mayor loading a Rig with drugs. Did y'all kill her when she found out what you were up to." Eric asked while shaking uncontrollably.

"I didn't do anything to your mom. I loved her. She was just in the wrong place at the wrong time. Pete Wilson had her kilt. They would've killed me too if I would've tried to stop him."

"A real man would've died trying to protect the woman that he loves. A real man would've never put the woman that he loves in that position. You a real fuck boy in my eyes. We ain't going to kill you though. We need you to get close to Pete. I plan on murdering him with my bare hands." Elihu used hand gestures showing how bad he wanted to take his life.

Jeff could see the hurt in Elihu's eyes. The camouflage outfit he was wearing added to the fact that he was ready for war. "I'll gladly turn him over to you," Jeff said while picking up the phone and calling Pete. Once he picked up Jeff asked him to meet with him. Which he gladly agreed.

"You two know what to do," Elihu stated to Venom and Snoop. Turning to his son next. "Get a couple of your most trusted brothers and see if they would ride for you. Something tells me that Pete ain't going to move around right now without a few guns with him. We need to be prepared for any situation." Elihu explained to them all before everyone went in their own direction. "Not you boss man. You staying with me." He said to Jeff stopping him dead in his tracks.

Jeff held his hands up as he took his seat back at the table. "So if you don't mind me asking. How did you guys get in the house from the back?"

"We took the door apart. Now chill out and get comfortable until its time to meet up with Pete." Elihu told him while he stood in the corner of the living room with his gun in his hand. If Jeff tried anything funny he planned to blow any thoughts of him escaping out of his mind.

Ten minutes later his satellite phone started ringing. Only two people called that phone. "What's good?" He said into the phone.

"Have you seen the news yet my friend? If you haven't you might wanna tune in." Gustavo jokingly said into the phone with the sound of heavy winds in the background.

Elihu quickly turned the television to channel 7 news. The headlines were of Gustavus Dominguez breakout from prison. His friend was free and on his way to Mexico.

"I guess I'll see you soon my friend. I just have one thing to wrap up here first. God speed my friend." Elihu said into the phone then ended the call. All he can think about was sky being the limit now that his friend has busted out of prison. His ties to Mexico are much stronger now.

CHAPTER SIXTEEN

Pete new that his days were numbered in Miami. Without Saudy and her drugs, his hold on the streets was no more. He just needs to take his show on the road. He could care less about running for Mayor any more. All he needed to do before he leaves is cut off all of his loose ins. He rounded up all the money that he had on the streets and the money that was stashed away in different safe deposit boxes around the city. A grand total of $2,300,000.00 rested in the trunk of his Benz.

When he got to the meet-up spot with ten of his best gunmen. He instructed them to kill Jeff on sight. What he didn't know was that they were surrounded. Elihu knew that he would come because he needed confirmation that Jeff was dead.

While Jeff slowly drove down the one way/dead end street Eric's gang brother's along with Venom and Snoop started taking out Pete's men. Pete didn't have a clue of any of these things taking place as he sat behind the wheel of his Benz. By there not being any street lights posted all Pete men were basically sitting ducks.

Trying not to alarm any of the goons while taking their time. Venom and Snoop crept up on Pete's goons and sliced their necks then gently placing their lifeless bodies down on the grass.

Once the ok was given to Jeff that there weren't any more hidden surprises did he exit his very own car. From where Elihu stood he could tell that Jeff was very shaken up.

Pete just knew he had a sitting duck. From all, he knew Jeff had come alone making things that much easier for his goons to take him out. With a smile on his face as he climbed from behind the wheel of his car. "So what do I owe for this meeting? How did you sleep last night, or did you get any at all?" He knows that he was wrong for adding salt on an open wound, but he could care less. Having people killed was nothing to him.

"You didn't have to kill her. You knew what she meant to me. You didn't give me a chance to talk to her. Maybe I could've talked her into keeping her mouth shut." Jeff snapped. He was furious and wanted Pete's blood for it.

Pete just chuckled. Jeff was a bitch and he knew it. "You better tone it down before you find yourself in the bottom of the ocean with your police ass wife. She would snitch, and you know it. Just like every other time she found one of them trailers she had flew off the deep end. Fuck am I having this conversation with your ass for. Kill his bitch ass." He called out to his goons and not one emerged from the thick bushes. "I said kill this fool!" He shouted out. A look of confusion displayed across his face. He was lost for words when Elihu's men emerged instead. "What the hell is going on?"

"What's going on. Your goons are dead. The tables have turned and you're standing here alone. How does it feel to be the one alone? It doesn't feel good right. It makes you feel powerless." Jeff added while slowly approaching Pete with the Glock that Elihu had given him in his hand. Lisa was his wife, so he felt the need to be the one to take Pete's life.

"Hold on now Jeff. You know I was just fucking around with you. We family and family would never kill each other. I was just trying to shake you up to keep you from having cold feet. Those men were for my protection in case you tried to harm me." Pete was just running on out the mouth trying to convince Jeff to think about what he was about to do.

Elihu stepped out from behind him with Saudy standing at his side. "Jeff be done with this fool. No more words are needed."

Pete followed the familiar voice until he was looking in the direction behind him. Standing before him was Elihu and Saudy on American soil. He never thought he'll see the day when she would risk coming into the states. Her presence alone secured his death was final. There was no way he was walking out of this one a live. "You replacing me with a jock. What does a football player knows about drugs? Saudy you going to seriously regret this."

"No what I regret is ever doing business with you. Get rid of him." She turned and told Elihu.

"Gladly!" He replied while motioning for Venom and Snoop to kill both Pete and Jeff.

Jeff never saw it coming. Snoop moved on him like a theft in the. Using his left arm to choke him out while stabbing him multiple times in the back over and over until he stops crying out from the pain. Pete on the other hand just dropped to his knees. He knew that there was no place for him to run. With his head hung low Venom stabbed him in the back of the neck jamming the blade so deep he was instantly paralyze. Before his body could hit the flow Venom had snatched the blade out and sliced his throat from ear to ear.

Saudy stopped for a second to admire the new piece of jewelry that rested around Elihu's neck. "So you a Don now? That's where I recognized this ring."

"I like to think of myself as the Boss of all Bosses. Those Don's ain't never seen a Don like me. With your grade A Coke I'm going to quickly lock down the whole east coast. Shit, look at my new team. We about to change the game." He said while proudly looking back at his new family. When he laid eyes on his only son he waved for him to join him with Saudy for a moment. "This here is my son. Half of the reason I go so hard. With his mom gone I'm all he and his sister have now. Eric meet Saudy. Your new God Mother."

She was flattered no one had never asked her to take on such a roll. The jester alone made her look at Elihu different. "I'm proud to be your kid's Godmother, whatever that means."

"I'll tell you all about it when I make my next trip to Mexico. But for now we have so much to discuss." He informed her as they made their exit leaving His men to split the money in Pete's trunk.

To be continued.....

EPILOGUE

City Girlz: The Come Up

CITY GIRLZ

The Come Up

Ms. Murphy's group home for teenage girls was a known place for girls with attitude problems, multiple criminal charges, and straight fuck-ups all together. There was a total of twenty girls in the house at all times. When one left, another one replaces her that same night. Ms. Murphy kicks the girls out the day they turn 18 years old. Her group home has been in business for over 25 years and counting. There has never been a case where Ms. Murphy broke her own rule. Shy knew that even if she wasn't ready, she didn't have a choice but to ready herself. In the morning, she'll be turning 18 years of age. Her girls helped her pack her things. She had three years to ready herself for the real world. Unlike most of the girls in the group home, she did apply herself in school, so she does have her high school diploma. Graduate from Miami North Western, home of the mighty Bulls.

Once all of Shy's things were packed, and Ms. Murphy was yelling for all the girls to turn the lights off, she and her three best friends stepped outside the back door. Each of the girls had tears in their eyes. Over the years, they have grown to be more than friends, they became sisters.

"Ok, ladies. The ball is ticking. We been preparing for this day. I'm going to start working at Burger King. Every two weeks, I'm going to make sure to send y'all back money for feminine things." Shy explained to them.

"Fuck all that. We know you ain't going to forget about us. I need you to hold shit down out there. We'll be home shortly after you." Qua said, trying not to enjoy her last moments with Shy discussing things that they had planned for months now.

"Hate to have to agree with this pistol, but she's right. What you pulled us outside for?" Amber asked while sticking her hands inside her pockets while trying to warm up.

"Yea, what's good, Shy?" Quan added in.

Shy pulled out the razor blade that she been hiding in her pocket. "Let's become blood sisters." both Quan & Qua gave her a look with their mouths twisted. "of course, we know that you two are twins. This is going to bring the four us together. Are y'all down?"

Everyone nodded in agreement while sticking out their right hand, palms up. Taking the blade, she lightly cut her own palm until it bled, then she made a circle starting with Amber, and ending with Qua.

"Now, all four of us can embrace in one handshake mixing the blood together."

They followed what Shy said, mixing each of their Blood together. Sharing a laugh once they broke up and headed in the house. They were caught off guard by Ms. Murphy standing there in the kitchen. They knew that they were in big trouble. After 9 o'clock lights supposed to go out, and everyone must be in their room.

"Shy, take a seat. The rest of you girls head to your room. I'll deal with y'all later." Ms. Murphy stood there a moment while waiting on the girls' room door to close. Once it did, she slowly crept up on Qua, knowing that she wouldn't go to bed without trying to hear what she had to tell Shy. "You want me to get you twice?"

"No, ma'am." She shouted out once she spotted Ms. Murphy. She could never pull a fast one on the old lady.

Shaking her head, not knowing what she was going to do with the twins. Once she got back to the table, she took a seat opposite of Shy. Before starting, she took a second to look Shy in the eyes. Smirking because she still remembers the day Shy stepped foot in her house. She was a lost little girl that didn't have any idea about the real world. The sad part was that Shy was still clueless. Out of all the teenage girls that came and passed through her house She had taken a real liking to Shy, but her rules were set in place for a reason. She was going to have to figure life out for herself in a flash or get washed up in the way of the world like the rest of the people that couldn't figure out how to make ends meet.

Shy didn't know what to expect from this sit down with Ms. Murphy. If she was in trouble, she wasn't wearing any ass beating tonight. Her days and nights of getting her ass beat were over with. In less than 3 hours, she'll be a grown woman.

Ms. Murphy took a clean washcloth and wiped the cut on Shy hand clean. She applied some ointment, then wrapped her hand up with a fresh wrap, then taped it down tight. "Tomorrow, you'll be leaving this house. You don't have to return for any visits because no one does." She paused for a moment as if she was thinking of something else to say. "Also, while you out there. You can apply for Hud housing or Section-8. I already signed you up for food stamps. On your way out in the morning, I'll give you an envelope with all your important documents. Once you walk out of this door in the morning, you'll be responsible for your own well-being. Please don't go out there, acting all scary. You gone have to put on your big girl panties and find your place in life. The world is a frigid place, and it'll eat you alive if you let it, and only the strongest survive." Ms. Murphy saw a strong woman when she looked at Shy, but she was rough around the edges, and also green as a pool table, and twice as square.

Shy didn't know how to respond to Ms. Murphy. Instead of opening her mouth and saying something stupid, she listened as Ms. Murphy dropped jewels on her.

"Once you out that door, you have to make every move your best move. Whatever happened with the Burger King job that you applied for?"

"I have to pick up my uniforms in the morning. I'll be alright though. I can't wait to start my life on my own." She said, trying to remain calm, knowing that she doesn't have a clue as to what life has for her outside of Ms. Murphy's home.

Ms. Murphy shook her head. She knows for a fact that Shy was doomed, but if Shy wanted to go about this the hard way, who was she to stop her. "I wish you the best of luck. Goodnight, Shy." Ms. Murphy patted Shy on top of her hand, then stood up to leave.

Shy sat there for a moment until Ms. Murphy was out of rear sight. Thinking to herself about what life has in store for her outside the door. Each time she tried to think about it, she'll only come up blank. Bursting into tears, she cried for a moment. Tears of fear and tears of joy at the same time. After only minutes, she wiped her eyes and face clean, then made her way to the room that she shared with her three best friends.

When she walked into the room, her three friends rushed to her aid, then they embraced in a group hug while crying together. All of their lives were about to change overnight.

Made in the USA
Monee, IL
02 June 2020